SMOKY MOUNTAIN TRACKS

A Raine Stockton Dog Mystery

Donna Ball

A SIGNET BOOK

SIGNET
Published by New American Library, a division of
Penguin Group (USA) Inc., 375 Hudson Street,
New York, New York 10014, USA
Penguin Group (Canada), 90 Eglinton Avenue East, Suite 700, Toronto,
Ontario M4P 2Y3, Canada (a division of Pearson Penguin Canada Inc.)
Penguin Books Ltd., 80 Strand, London WC2R 0RL, England
Penguin Ireland, 25 St. Stephen's Green, Dublin 2,
Ireland (a division of Penguin Books Ltd.)
Penguin Group (Australia), 250 Camberwell Road, Camberwell, Victoria 3124,
Australia (a division of Pearson Australia Group Pty. Ltd.)
Penguin Books India Pvt. Ltd., 11 Community Centre, Panchsheel Park,
New Delhi - 110 017, India
Penguin Group (NZ), cnr Airborne and Rosedale Roads, Albany,
Auckland 1310, New Zealand (a division of Pearson New Zealand Ltd.)
Penguin Books (South Africa) (Pty.) Ltd., 24 Sturdee Avenue,
Rosebank, Johannesburg 2196, South Africa

Penguin Books Ltd., Registered Offices:
80 Strand, London WC2R 0RL, England

First published by Signet, an imprint of New American Library,
a division of Penguin Group (USA) Inc.

First Printing, March 2006
10 9 8 7 6 5 4 3 2 1

Chapter One

If there's one thing I've learned in my thirty-odd (sometimes very odd) years of life, it's that nothing good ever happens at three o'clock in the morning. Well, okay, sometimes someone has a baby, or a litter of puppies, but since no one I knew was expecting either, and since anyone who knew me understood that no matter how excited *they* were about the news, I would be much more likely to receive it in the spirit it was meant after sunrise, I had no reason to expect to hear anything that would make me happy when the phone rang at 3:06 A.M.

I was right.

I spent a few moments trying not to choke on my own adrenaline as the first couple of rings jolted me up on my elbows in bed and pounded panic through my head, and another few trying to find my voice and read the blurry numbers on the clock.

When by that time it appeared that whoever was on the line was not going to hang up, I fumbled the phone off the hook and croaked—foolishly trying to sound as though I had not been asleep for the past four hours—"Hello, this is Raine."

"Hey."

A voice that needed no introduction.

And because he was no dummy, he added quickly, "Don't hang up. Look, we've got a situation out here and we need a team. I just talked to Hank Baker and he said to give you a call. Can you get over to the bridge at Three Mile Creek in half an hour?"

About halfway through his speech I decided to actually bring the phone, which had been on its way to its cradle, back to my ear, so I only missed part of what he said. Still, I hated how stupid I sounded as I said, still croaking, "What?"

Of course, he wasn't going to win any Mensa awards for his reply. "You awake?" He sounded tolerant and amused and just a tad condescending—the way you speak to a child whose feelings you don't want to hurt.

"Yeah, Buck," I snapped back wittily, "I was just sitting here painting my toenails and waiting for my pizza delivery. What the hell's the matter with you, calling me at this hour? You know I'm not on the list anymore. Hank knows it too. Call the prison."

Again, I caught his voice as the phone was

halfway from my ear to the cradle. "We did, but it'll take them three hours to get their dogs here, and by that time it'll be daylight. Hank is coming but he's an hour and a half away."

I hesitated. "I don't have a dog."

The trouble with Buck was that he had known me far too long and could read my silences far too well. He knew when to push, and how.

"What's wrong with Cisco?"

"He's never been field-tested. We haven't even been to class in six months."

I don't know why I didn't just hang up the phone and start putting on my clothes. I think I must've known how this conversation was going to end the minute I heard his voice.

"I thought he was certified."

"Tested," I corrected. "He passed the tracking-dog test, but that's a lot different from doing SAR work. He's only two years old—"

"Look, Raine," Buck said and lowered his voice a fraction in a way that might have been meant to convey urgency, or perhaps confidentiality. "We've got a woman and a child missing. It's thirty-six degrees out here and that little girl's coat was still hanging on a hook by the door. We need a tracking dog and we need it now. What are you going to do?"

I felt a kind of tightening in my chest, a squeezing off of emotions, even as I closed my eyes,

tightly, trying to block out the picture of a small coat hanging by the door and shards of ice crystals— they called it dog ice—forming in the muddy tracks on the ground. It had to be a child. Of course it had to be a child. He would never have called me other wise.

I said, with as little expression as possible, "God-damn you, Buck."

He said, "I'll meet you at the bridge."

I hung up the phone and started pulling on my clothes. The squeezing in my chest didn't go away. It never did when there was a child involved. I hated these kinds of cases; I just hated them.

But these kinds of cases were exactly why I did what I did.

Due to what the papers call "recent events," a lot of attention has been placed on SAR—search and rescue—dogs lately, and that's as it should be. But it can also be a little confusing. The way the media sometimes makes it look, there are whole platoons of these highly skilled dogs and their handlers standing by, ready to fly anywhere in the world to dig through fallen rubble, track through avalanches, dive for corpses. And, indeed, there are a few pro-fessionally organized groups in the United States that, in fact, almost fit that description. But mostly we're just a bunch of people with great dogs, loosely aligned through tracking clubs, who picked up a hobby that can sometimes save lives. We meet

once a month or once a week to practice with our dogs in simulated rescue situations. We take specialized training in first aid and search techniques. When we have been tested and proven, we usually register with local law enforcement as an emergency SAR team. It's like being a volunteer firefighter, only, thank God, our services are not usually needed so often.

Up here it's mostly wilderness rescue—the occasional hiker who drifts off the Appalachian Trail, a tourist (or, as we like to say, a damn fool tourist) who thinks he knows all about backwoods camping, a child or an elderly person who gets confused and wanders into the woods. Sometimes we find them; sometimes we don't. Sometimes they find themselves. Sometimes they are found by another hiker, or a hunter, or a dog . . . next spring, when it's too late.

I have lived in these mountains all my life, and one thing I know for sure: Nature is in charge here, and she's not always friendly. We are just visitors in her domain, and it doesn't hurt to remind ourselves of that every now and then.

I got involved with Hank Baker some ten years back because I'm a sucker for a compliment. Somebody said to me, "Your dog has a great nose on her. You really ought to do something with her." In fact Cassidy *did* have a great nose—she had a great everything—and tracking turned out to be only one

of half a dozen activities we enjoyed doing together. Before I knew it, I had been drawn into the whole world of dogs and dog sports. Search and rescue was a big part of that world—partly because of Hank and partly because of the fact that I live at the very edge of one of the densest sections of national forest in the country, where there is a more-than-common need for it.

But, as I had told Buck, I don't do it much anymore. I rarely even made it to class. And now, as I double knotted my heavy-duty hikers and tossed the contents of my sweater drawer looking for my working gloves, I couldn't imagine what had gotten into me, agreeing to do this. Why wasn't I back in bed, chasing off the predawn chill with three layers of Granny Applewaite's homemade quilts? Why didn't I call Buck back on his cell and tell him to wait for the goddamn prison dogs?

Why had I even answered the phone?

I found my gloves and took another two minutes to brush my teeth and run a wide-toothed comb through my mass of short, tightly wound brown curls. I opened the bedroom door and almost tripped over Cisco, who was sleeping flat on his back with his paws up in the air, glommed so closely onto my door that, if he could have turned himself into liquid gold, he would have oozed through the crack beneath it and into the room.

Usually my dogs are crated at night. I think it's

better for them to have a secure place of their own in which to sleep, and certainly it's better for me. But Cisco had never crated well—among his other oddities, he had this weird claustrophobia thing about being confined—and, except for his fantasy about belonging in my bedroom, he did just fine sleeping loose in the house at night. With one very notable exception, my beloved Cassidy, I had never allowed dogs in my bedroom. After two years, Cisco had finally begun to accept that, if not to understand it.

He rolled over when I opened the door, gave me an abashed, unhurried grin, and got to all fours, shaking out his golden fur and executing a lovely, wide-yawned, three-point stretch, curling his white-feathered tail over his back and placing his magnificent head between his paws. Cisco—aka Summertime's Cassidy Rides Again, NAJ, TD—was truly a magnificent specimen and a credit to his breeding, with the exception of a few little peculiarities, as I have mentioned. But as anyone who has ever lived with a golden retriever knows, the first three years are the hardest. He was two years, two months and six days old, and he had a lot to learn. Which did absolutely nothing to explain why an otherwise mostly sane person would be taking him into the dark woods in the middle of the night and trusting him to find two lost people.

I said, "Okay, boy, good stretch, let's go!"

He gave me a happy, expectant look that had "Breakfast!" written all over it, and bounded down the stairs after me.

The other three dogs—all rescued from neglectful or abusive circumstances, and all, through absolutely no fault of my own, having decided their best bet was to spend their remaining days here with me—slept soundly in their crates in the parlor. My mother had once held a luncheon for the wives of the state supreme court in that parlor; I did not like to think how fast she would turn over in her grave to see dog crates there now.

My mother's mantelpiece, which in her day had displayed silver candlesticks and china vases overflowing with lilacs, was now adorned with an oil painting of a golden retriever, a banner of AKC ribbons, and more than a dozen trophies. Her brocade settee was covered with sheets to keep the dog hair off, and her oriental rugs had long since been stored in the attic.

My name is Raine Stockton. I am thirty-three, five foot four, 120 pounds. Short, curly brown hair that tends to be a little out of control, round face, big brown eyes. Not entirely unattractive, but no beauty queen either. I was raised to be a genteel southern lady, the daughter of a respected district court judge and the president of the local chapter of the Daughters of the Confederacy. Neither one of them should be blamed for the way I turned out.

At this point, however, I would like to make one thing clear: I am not one of those crazy dog people. You know, the ones who only own two kinds of outfits: sweats with scruffy Reeboks and jeans with scruffy Reeboks. They always smell like the cheese they use for training treats, and they wear clickers around their necks and wrists instead of jewelry. They mortgage their homes to buy the RVs that will take them to every dog show on the circuit, and while you'd be hard-pressed to find a copy of *Time* or *Newsweek* in their homes, they own every copy of *Clean Run* and *Front and Finish* ever published. They don't wear lipstick, and they wash their hair with Mane 'n Tail. They will blow off their sister's wedding for an agility trial without a second thought, and they never invite anyone to dinner who does *not* like dog hair in her food.

In my real life I am a consultant for the Forest Service, which is actually just a fancy way of saying I got to keep my job after government cutbacks reduced the local office staffing from three to two officers. I have a degree in wildlife biology, which qualifies me to fill in for vacations and emergencies and occasionally do some actual consulting work. For the past two years the income from my real job has been slightly over five thousand dollars. Good thing I had a backup plan.

In my life I have loved one dog and been fascinated and amused by a great many others. As it

turns out, I have a little talent for training them. Between that and the small boarding kennel I operate, I manage to keep my head above water most years. But I have lots of cute outfits and I wear lipstick at least once a week. And I try very hard not to smell like cheese.

I peeked in on the sleeping pups briefly, without turning on the light, on my way to the kitchen, where Cisco did not, in fact, get breakfast. There are many excellent reasons for not feeding a working dog before he goes to work, but the most important one at that hour of the morning was that I couldn't face the prospect of dishing up the oatmeal and chicken hearts that comprised his breakfast. I nonetheless tossed a sandwich bag full of freeze-dried liver treats into my pack, along with a banana and a granola bar for myself, and grabbed four bottles of water from the fridge. Everything else—first aid kit, dog toy, space blanket, matches, flashlight, flares, two-way radio—was already packed. Funny how I had kept the pack supplied, even though I knew I'd never be doing this kind of work again. Habit, I guess.

It wasn't until Cisco saw me grab his fluorescent orange SAR vest that he began to dance around the kitchen in excitement, dashing toward the door where his leash hung on a peg, spinning back to me again. Talk about a good work ethic. It had been months since we'd been on an early-morning train-

10

ing practice, but he seemed to remember. I guess it was habit with him too.

I took a minute to scribble a note to Maude, who would be in at seven to feed the dogs, then I opened the door and uttered the long-awaited words: "Okay, load up."

Cisco dashed out into the night toward the truck like a firefighter down a ladder. Not a bad comparison, all things considered. I was right behind him. We were pulling out of the yard and headed toward the highway twelve minutes after I hung up the phone.

Chapter Two

I live in what might well be the most beautiful place in the world. Let the devil have his craggy peaks and purple deserts; when people talk about God's country, this is what they mean. Deep in the heart of a Smoky Mountain glade on a still, cool, spring afternoon, you can hear the muffled beat of drums, you can smell the smoke of laurel campfires and you are transported back in time a hundred years, a thousand. Breathe deep of the sweet green air after a sudden rainstorm and you will know what the world smelled like on the first day of creation. Beauty here is dark and lush and ancient, and it's something you not so much see as feel.

My family has inhabited this little piece of paradise since 1852, and for the most part none of us has ever wanted to be anywhere else. I wake up every morning with the Nantahala Forest on one side of

me and the Blue Ridge Mountains on the other. My dogs play in a stream that's so clear you can see the trout dashing and darting between their paws. Every evening I walk down to the edge of the property and lose myself in the sound of a waterfall that cascades down thirty feet of timeworn boulders and I ask myself how I could possibly be so lucky as to live in such a place.

In May the meadows are yellow with clover and the woods redolent of sweetshrub. In June and July the roadsides are a fairyland of deep pink rhododendron and lacy laurel, and there is nothing more majestic than the evergreens weighed down with snow in the crisp white heart of the winter when incredible tricks of high-country light make it seem as though you can see deer playing on mountain trails a hundred miles away.

But in the dead-cold grip of a March night, hours before dawn, there is nothing bleaker, nothing more grim, than what the ravages of winter have left behind on the edge of the forest. Tangled deadfalls from the most recent ice storm littered the sides of the road, and the broken spines of hardwood trees jutted out from the woods. The Explorer bounced over frozen mud ruts and the headlights swayed across the crooked fingers of low-hanging limbs. I turned up the heater full blast and still could see my breath in the cold. The night was so deep, and so black, that I might well have been the only person

living on the planet. I knew for certain that I was the only one moving.

I live about five miles from Hansonville, a good-sized little town whose population can swell to over three thousand in the summer and fall, and which, even at this time of year, leaves the streetlights on all night. It boasts a McDonald's, a Waffle House, and a twenty-four-hour gas station, all of which spread little pools of light and warmth across the highway, along with the scent of coffee and the promise of civilization. But I was moving west, away from town, past hulking, shadowed trailer homes, deserted RV parks and dead-dark fescue fields, and there was not a light to be seen.

That situation ended abruptly when I turned off Old Highway 16 and onto Three Mile Creek Road. I could see the pulse of blue lights a mile away, and as I approached the bridge I found the road blocked by three police cars. Two more were parked along the shoulder, all of them with lights rotating and radios crackling. I pulled the Explorer in behind one of them and cautiously got out.

It looked as though every member of the Hanover County Sheriff's Department had gathered at the roadside that night. Just looking at a night split by flashing blue lights and khaki uniforms was enough to make anyone's heart pound a little faster, and I had unwittingly plunged myself into the thick of it. My pulse was slamming in my

throat, and I was so busy trying to appear confident as I opened the tailgate and started gathering my gear that I didn't notice Buck break away from the crowd and start toward us. I also forgot to give Cisco a "stay" command—not that it necessarily would have made a difference. Cisco is the only dog I have ever had who has failed the Canine Good Citizen test twice, and he loved Buck Lawson beyond all reason. The minute he spotted Buck moving toward us he bolted from the car and ran toward his idol like a runaway freight train, pouncing on him with an ecstatic joy that all but knocked the full-grown police officer to the ground.

My preferred method of dealing with that kind of public misbehavior is a cool "I meant to do that" approach; it might not win me any dog-training awards, but it spares embarrassment all around. So while Buck returned Cisco's enthusiastic greeting, I calmly gathered our equipment from the back and waited until Buck and Cisco had already started toward me before turning and saying calmly, "Cisco, here." I had his harness in one hand and his SAR vest in the other, and when Cisco saw them he raced away from Buck and skidded into a perfect sit before me, panting happily up at me. Voilà: a perfectly trained dog.

Buck said, "Thanks for coming."

I busied myself by fastening Cisco into his harness and vest. The cold March night found the open

front of my unzipped jacket and sucked the heat from my core. I let my frozen fingers linger near the puffs of Cisco's breath to warm them. "Like you gave me any choice."

"Yeah, well . . ." He sounded uncomfortable and I glanced up at him suspiciously. His hands were stuffed into the pockets of his jacket, his head ducked against the cold, and in the eerie, uncertain light his expression was unreadable. "It'll probably amount to nothing, but there are a couple of things I didn't mention on the phone."

Already I didn't like the sound of this. I straightened up warily, looping Cisco's leash around my hand. "Like what?"

"What I mean is, we'll probably find them both safe and sound at her mother's or something—"

"Well, what in the world did you drag me out of bed in the middle of the night for, then?" I demanded, exasperated.

He was spared further explanation by a call from over his shoulder and we both looked to see Sheriff Bleckley approaching—or, as I preferred to call him, Uncle Roe.

His real name was Richard Orson—R.O.—but it had been shortened to Roe at some point in the long-forgotten past and no one had called him anything else since. He had been sheriff as long as I could remember, which is not unusual in rural com-

munities. People like to know who their friends—or enemies—are, and they don't take well to change.

He rubbed his hands together and blew streams of frosty breath across the night as he approached. "Hey there, Rainbow," he said, and I tried not to wince. That was the disadvantage of having relatives strewn halfway around the county—you never could quite escape those childhood nicknames.

He was bald and a little on the round side, and in the cold his ears and nose were bright red. The Bleckleys, of which my mother had been one, had a way about them: kind of mild and easygoing, and it wasn't easy to tell what they were thinking most of the time. Nothing indicated how worried Uncle Roe really was except two small lines at the corners of his eyes.

"I guess Buck filled you in," he said.

I snapped Cisco back into a sit as he started to lunge toward the newcomer. "Not exactly."

Roe glanced at Buck but didn't waste time with nonessential questions or comments. With a jerk of his head, he indicated that we should walk while he talked, and we started back toward the cars.

"About an hour ago we got a call from over on Farmer's Road—Cindy Winston's neighbors. You know Cindy, works down at the Waffle House. Her mama's Hazel Winston, does sewing on the side."

I said shortly, "I know her."

He looked at me with his typically unreadable Bleckley features, and he was probably figuring out just *how* I knew her—or rather knew of her. Cindy Winston and I traveled in slightly different circles, but we did appear to have had one thing in common at one point in our lives: the man I had once been foolish enough to marry. Or so rumor had it. Rumor also had it that Cindy had lots of men in common with lots of women, and whether or not any of that was true hardly mattered to me at this point.

Roe resumed abruptly, "Anyway, neighbors said they heard yelling, then gunfire. Considering who that young lady's taken to hanging out with, it didn't sound too good, so we dispatched a car over to the trailer park. Her door's standing open, lights all on, neighbors swear they seen Luke Pickens' pickup truck hightail it out of there not five minutes before. Blood on the floor," he added tersely, without glancing at me, "and this."

We had reached the sheriff's car, and he opened the door. From inside he pulled a ziplock bag with what looked like a fuzzy stuffed toy inside. On closer examination I saw that it was a child's pink bedroom slipper with a bunny's head and ears making up the toe. It was speckled with something that looked like mud, but it wasn't. It was tiny drops of blood. My stomach roiled.

Hearing about a crime is one thing, but seeing a

baby's fuzzy bunny slipper splattered with blood is another one altogether.

"Just one?" I managed.

He nodded. "It must've fallen off when she was being carried out. Her coat was still hanging up. We're trying to get hold of somebody to find out if she had more than one coat, but chances are she's out here with one shoe and no coat. Truck's down there." He nodded toward a steep decline on the far side of the bridge. "The way it's resting, looks like somebody drove it off the road on purpose. There's blood in the truck bed."

I stared at him. There's probably a reason I didn't go into law enforcement, and it might just be because even at my best I've never been all that good at putting together puzzles. At three o'clock in the morning, it was pointless to even try.

"Okay," I ventured anyway, after a moment. "So you're saying that what we're really looking for out here is three people, and one of them is crazy Luke Pickens and he's got a gun?"

I was dismayed by Roe's slow, unhappy nod. "He might've thought he'd have a better chance hiding the truck here and trying to cut across the mountain to Tennessee. From what we can put together, he probably shot Cindy. Maybe she got away from him, and maybe she's got the kid. Or maybe she didn't get away, and he's got the girl."

"Maybe the reason he drove the truck off the

road was to dump a body," I said because I wanted him to know I hadn't overlooked the obvious.

"Maybe. But what we know for sure is somebody's hurt, and the kid has got to be out here somewhere."

"And Luke has a gun," I repeated, just in case he'd missed it the first time.

Roe said, "He's got to know he's screwed up bad this time, or he wouldn't have gone on the run. If he's trying to make it across the mountain, he's not going to be slowed down by a woman and child. They're out here."

I gazed down at Cisco worriedly. He was sniffing every frostbitten blade of grass and muddy frozen footprint in an absolute ecstacy of tracking-dog delight, which made my words a little less than persuasive when I muttered uncomfortably, "I'm not sure we're the right team for the job."

Roe replied dismissively, as though it were a matter of record, "You're the best."

No, I wanted to cry angrily, *I'm not. My dog was! I never knew what I was doing out there; it was Cassidy who did it all.*

But of course I didn't say anything of the sort, partly because that was the last thing he needed to hear right then, and partly because when I looked at him I realized that what he meant was, *You're all we've got.*

"I've got enough deputies covering these woods

to flush every possum in the state," he added reassuringly, "and every one of them has a gun."

He reached back inside the squad car and brought out a framed photograph. "This is her. It's probably a couple of years old. We're trying to get a more recent photo from the grandmother."

I glanced at the picture, which really wasn't necessary for my work—after all, if I found a child in the woods at three in the morning I would assume she needed help, whether or not she matched the photo—but then I stared. The little girl had short, pale hair and a solemn expression, and her arms were around a big, grinning golden retriever in a Santa hat. Pain sliced through my heart and sank to my stomach. I had to swallow a couple of times before I could speak, and I still couldn't take my eyes off the photo.

"I think I know her," I said. Cindy Winston's little girl. I had never known her name, never had any reason to. Small world. Small town.

Roe nodded. "I thought that was your dog."

Every year, as one of our therapy dog activities, Cassidy and I had done a little program for the children at Head Start on pet care and training; it was the highlight of the school year, if I do say so myself. We always went just before the Christmas break, and Cassidy would carry a basket filled with candy that she passed out to the kids. She showed them her counting trick while I talked about how impor-

tant it was to pay attention in school. She sang a few choruses of "Jingle Bells"—which sounded a lot like "Woof-woof-woof"—and then fetched a present from under the tree for each child. For a grand finale, each child got to have a Polaroid snapshot taken with "Santa Dog."

There were dozens of these photos with Cassidy scattered over the county, each one featuring a different three- or four-year-old face. I don't know what made me remember this particular child, unless it was that hers was one of the last photos with Santa Dog ever made. Or maybe it had something to do with how that earnest little face never cracked a smile as she wrapped her arms tightly around Cassidy's neck and assured me gravely, "Someday I'm gonna have a dog just like this one."

Someday.

"What's her name?" I asked, more softly than I had intended.

"Angel. Angel Winston."

"All right," I said gruffly, tearing my eyes away from the photo at last. "Let's take a look at the search grid."

Chapter Three

It has been said that every woman deserves one good man in her lifetime, and one good dog. I haven't yet found the one good man, but I've already had my one good dog.

Her name was CH Summertime's Sundance Kid, CDX, MACH, MXJ, TDX, VCD, CGC, TDI, 2001 North Carolina Companion Dog of the Year, call name Cassidy. In her thirteen years of life she made fifteen "finds"—successful conclusions to a search and rescue mission. That might not be a record, but it is definitely worth noting. She excelled in obedience, agility and tracking dog competitions. She was a certified therapy dog with more than one hundred visits to schools, hospitals and nursing homes. She was my heart.

Her last search was a good one. A young couple camping in the Nantahala had apparently wan-

dered off the marked hiking trail and become lost. They had been missing for almost two days before we were called in. I wasn't too happy about taking a dog of Cassidy's age on such a rigorous search, but what choice did I have? People's lives were at stake. And when I look back on it, I realize Cassidy wouldn't have had it any other way.

It was July, and contrary to what one might think, it gets hot in the mountains in July. It was a miserable search, filled with briars and biting insects and one or two rattlesnakes who fortunately were not in the mood for confrontation and slithered out of our way before any harm was done. Cassidy had a little bit of arthritis in her left hip, and by the afternoon of the second day she was limping badly. I wanted to take her home, but there is a certain bond that develops between a working dog and a handler; you almost start to read your dog's thoughts. Cassidy did not want to go home. She would have been humiliated if I had called her off. She was on a trail. And so, limping and panting and sweltering in the heat, she kept going. And by sunset we found the wife, who had been pinned by the ankle beneath a fallen rock. Her husband, who had started to hike out for help, was found by another team a couple of hours later.

The woman was dehydrated and feverish, and it is safe to say that if Cassidy had not found her when

she did, she might not have survived another night in the wild.

Exhausted and content, Cassidy rested her head in my lap as the sheriff's Jeep drove us off the mountain. Half-asleep myself, I tangled my hand in her fur and closed my eyes. I remember that she heaved one great sigh, and she did not breathe again.

Cassidy, Summertime's Sundance Kid, died as she had lived: a hero. There would never be another dog like her. And I would never be the same without her.

But because there was a child's life involved, I had to try.

Half the skill of working a tracking dog is handling the line. When you're doing it in the frozen, black woods, clambering over deadfalls and ice-slick boulders, ploughing through shallow creek beds and stands of brambles, it becomes less a skill than a mad, desperate dance to stay on your feet.

Roe let Cisco examine the bunny slipper to his heart's content (although in my opinion Cisco was much too young and inexperienced to have any useful scent-discrimination abilities), in hopes that he would be able to pick that scent out of the hundreds of thousands of others that infused the forest. I figured it couldn't hurt. Once given the command to track, Cisco was off like a bullet, his nose to the

ground, crisscrossing the scent pattern, dashing back to double-check, occasionally pausing to scent the air. He certainly looked like he knew what he was doing. But what, exactly, he was tracking was anybody's guess.

We worked in teams of three, with my team in the lead so as to allow Cisco as uncontaminated a scent trail as possible. The night was dotted with flashlight beams and the muffled crackle of trampling feet. Buck was on my left, and Wyn Rogers, one of Hanover County's three female police officers, on my right. Their radios were turned down so as not to obscure a call for help from a weakened victim, should there be one, and the muted static mingled with the sound of our labored breathing and Cisco's paws scrambling through crisp, frozen leaves. This was not easy terrain, and two steep hills, three frozen streams, and one long, flat deer trail had passed before anyone had the breath to waste on conversation.

Buck edged close to me and said in what might have passed for a casual tone had it not been so strained with exertion, "Look, I hope you don't think this was my idea."

"Don't be ridiculous."

"Roe made me call you."

"I know who you take your orders from."

"Because if you think for one minute—"

"This is a stupid conversation."

"So I noticed."

Cisco made a sudden bound forward and I left Buck behind.

"What do you think?" Wyn puffed, catching up with me. "Do you think he's got anything?"

"It's hard to say." I tried to sound authoritative, which is not easy when you're gasping for breath. "Scent is a funny thing, especially in this weather. If hunters were out last night or even yesterday morning, there could be enough of their scent left to pull him onto their trail. And we're getting pretty close to Jim Peterson's place. He might've been out here cutting firewood or something. You just never know."

"But, I mean, he couldn't just be chasing a deer or a raccoon or something, could he?"

Please, God, no, I thought, and answered with more confidence than I felt, "He's trained to track human scent. If they're out here, and I don't know how they couldn't be, the chances are pretty good that he's going to pick up on them."

Then I had to add, with an unhappy glance toward Buck, "Of course, a search like this is tough enough when the victim *wants* to be found. If they're being hidden, or—"

Suddenly Cisco veered sharply to the left and I had to scramble to keep up. I let the coarse cotton line slide through my fingers when I saw the plumy white tail in front of me take a downward slope. I

managed to crest the small rise without tripping over anything or unintentionally jerking my dog off the trail, but I wasn't agile enough to keep my feet on the descent. I slid the last few feet on the seat of my jeans, but Cisco was so intent on investigating the ground that even my abrupt arrival didn't cause him to look up.

"You okay?"

Buck arrived just as I was brushing off my soggy backside and regaining control of my flashlight. I nodded and turned my attention back to Cisco.

"Has he got something?" Wyn added her light to ours and for a moment Cisco, nose down and tail waving wildly, was the star of his own floodlit stage.

"Maybe," I said, "but probably not. Scent tends to pool in low places, especially on nights like this. They might have stopped here. Or they could be anywhere up there." I swung my light up and around the mountainous slopes that surrounded us on three sides.

Apparently satisfied with his investigations, Cisco bounded toward me for further instructions or, more likely, a treat. Buck went forward to do a visual search of the ground but reported after only a few minutes, "Nothing that I can see." He stood and brushed debris off his gloves. "But just in case, we'll have a better look in the daylight."

He took a small flag from his pocket and spent

some time trying to work the stake into the frozen ground. I looked once again up at the steep, bramble-covered slopes that surrounded us and thought in dismay how long it would take to search every inch of them . . . even in daylight, even with a dozen dogs and helicopters and even if the victims stayed exactly where they were until we found them, which victims never did. Then I thought about the grave-faced little girl and the golden retriever she might never get a chance to have, and I bent down abruptly and skimmed my hand over the ground in the familiar signal. "Cisco, track," I commanded.

He took off in a straight line, nose to the ground, and he didn't slow down until, a few hundred half-running steps later, a string of barbed wire forced him to stop and wait for me. We see enough barbed wire in these woods that it was worth teaching Cisco to stop all forward motion when he encountered it, and fortunately for him, that was one lesson he'd had no trouble learning.

I recognized the fence as part of a rambling enclosure that ran along the edge of Jim Peterson's farm. Fifty years ago they'd kept livestock here, but now most of the wires had popped or been cut by impatient hunters, or the trees around which the wire was wound had fallen. At this particular section only the middle wire was still intact, and I held it to the ground with my foot while I sent Cisco over. He took off quickly.

Wyn and Buck caught up with us less than ten steps later, and I think we all realized where we were heading at the same time. My eyes met Buck's in the reflected light of our combined flashes, but he was the one who spoke. "The old home place," he said.

My throat was tight with excitement and my voice came out sounding a little strained. "I think so. But stay back. Don't pull him off."

He gave me the kind of look I usually give him, the one that says, "How stupid do you think I am?" but I could tell he was checking his stride in an effort not to take the shortcuts that would lead him to the place he was certain Cisco was taking us.

"The home place?" Wyn questioned, keeping up with us. "You mean the one you can see from the highway?"

I had forgotten that Wyn had not grown up here. "No, that's the Petersons' house. We're talking about the old log cabin, the one that was built when their folks first settled here. We all used to play out there as kids. It was falling down even then. I can't believe . . ."

Then it came into view, at first just a darker shape in the darkness, and then the powerful reach of our flashlight beams picked out the stacked log walls, a half-fallen roof and the gaping hole where a door had once been. You couldn't have asked for a better

place to hide, or to hide someone . . . or to set up an ambush.

Cisco was eager now, covering the ground in great, happy leaps, and I had to run to keep up. "Easy!" I cautioned at just about the same moment Buck grabbed my arm, his hand on his holster. "Wait," he said.

We both might as well have saved our breath. When Buck pulled me back, Cisco pulled forward, and the line slipped through my fingers. I said, "Crap!" and lunged after him, but he was already through the door. I hadn't gone two more running steps before I heard it: a single, sharp, staccato bark.

Buck pushed me back and I swore at him, but Wyn blew past me on the other side, blocking my way. Both of them approached the building at a crouch with their guns out, like a couple of TV cops, and Wyn called, "Cindy? Angel?"

Another bark was the reply, and they disappeared inside. I was only a couple of steps behind them.

Some dogs are trained to return to the handler when they make a find, often carrying in their mouths a small stick that's attached to their collars to signal that they've been successful. Others are trained to bark, or paw at the ground, or lie down. Cisco had been trained to sit when he had made his find; adding the bark had been his own idea.

Cisco was in fact sitting when I went through the

door, but what he had found was not exactly what I expected. His tail was swishing back and forth, and his muzzle was buried halfway in a baked bean can.

"Cisco, leave it!" I shouted.

He started at the sound of my voice and looked guiltily over his shoulder at me with the can still attached to his muzzle. Then he pawed it off and gave it one last, loving lick before I snatched it up.

Buck reholstered his gun and said into the radio, "Um, that's a negative on the alert, Base." I could hear the amusement in his voice, and Wyn was working hard not to grin as she swung her beam around the empty room. "We'll check it out anyway, but looks like a false alarm."

Cisco was bounding around me, grinning like an idiot and trying to get at the pack where I kept the toy that was his reward for a good find. "Cisco, wrong," I said sharply. "You don't get rewarded for finding garbage." When he insisted, even going so far as to paw my pants leg, I took him firmly by the collar and held him still, glaring at him. "Go," I told him in my coldest "I mean business" tone, "lie down." I gestured angrily toward a corner, and he went reluctantly across the dirt floor, where he flopped down in the corner and began to whine softly.

I finished inspecting the can for toxic substances, or at least those that might be more toxic than weeks-old baked beans, and tossed it away. Cisco

raised his head but didn't dare run after it. "Careful there, sport," Buck said, playing his light over the sagging roof timbers. "That's evidence you're playing around with."

"Very funny." My cheeks were hot with annoyance and, if I was perfectly honest, no small amount of humiliation. No one likes to be made a fool of by her dog. The seat of my jeans, where I had fallen in the mud, was practically frozen to my rear, my boots were soaked clear through and my fingers were numb. I couldn't believe we'd just been dragged across country in the middle of the night for the sake of baked beans. "I told you he was too young."

"Come on, give the guy a break." Buck poked at the ashes of a long-dead fire with the toe of his boot. "Somebody's been here, just not recently. Hunters, probably, or kids smoking pot. You see anything, Wyn?"

"Nah. Damn, could it get any colder?"

Cisco was still whining, and I snapped at him, "Quiet!"

Buck said, "I'll check around outside."

Wyn and I met him in front of the building, shivering, when he returned with a negative report. I held Cisco by the collar, still not quite ready to forgive him. It was almost five o'clock in the morning, for God's sake. I had the right to be a little testy.

"We'll cut across the creek," Buck said, "and

head on back. Hank should be here soon with his dogs, and we've got two forest service helicopters on the way. No point in us freezing our butts off any longer than we have to. Our shift's just about over anyway."

I knew perfectly well that their shift didn't end until seven, and that neither one of them would go home until the victims were found. They just wanted to get rid of me, and I just wanted to go home.

We trudged through the woods for another twenty minutes, Wyn and Buck making desultory conversation about things like coffee and the heater in their patrol car, which was broken. Not that I blamed them; warm things were first and foremost on my mind too. But it always amazed me the way cops did that—relegated the crises of death and dying to a mere job, and managed somehow still to have a relatively normal life.

Okay, I had been in search and rescue for a few years myself. I knew we didn't always get our man. But damn it, this time I had really wanted it. I had really wanted that little blond-haired girl to have her picture taken for the newspaper with her arms around Cisco. *Someday I'm gonna have a dog just like this one.*

Well, there. That's what vanity will get you.

And you see, that's how I managed to do the work that I did and still have a relatively normal

life. I didn't think about the alternatives. I didn't consider the consequences of failure. Someone would find her. It just wouldn't be me.

"Goddamn it," I muttered out loud and came to an abrupt halt. Cisco, who, to his credit, had been paying particularly close attention to me since the incident at the cabin, sat automatically when I stopped.

I had been so wrapped up in my own morose thoughts that I hadn't noticed that we had come to the footbridge that crossed Three Mile Creek. It was not much more than a dead fall, really, two trees that had been cut to lie across the shallowest part of the creek and that had since been reinforced with the debris and detritus of a constantly moving waterway. It was a little narrow, but sturdy enough. Buck and Wyn had already crossed it and were waiting for me on the other bank.

But here's the thing. Cisco has issues with bridges. In SAR training, there is the crossover with baffles, which is designed to teach dogs to carefully negotiate debris piles while precisely placing their feet for proper balance. In agility, there is the dog-walk, a similarly constructed device that is composed of an up ramp, a down ramp, and a connecting ramp that the dog is expected to cross at full speed. Cisco, never the most graceful pup, had taken bad falls from both pieces of equipment in

training and was having a hard time getting over them. To his way of thinking, all bridges were traps.

Still, Wyn and Buck were watching, and after the fiasco with the baked beans I felt obliged to give it the old college try.

"Cisco, walk it," I commanded brightly and tugged on his leash.

His rump remained firmly planted on the ground.

"Walk it," I insisted, tugging harder.

He rolled his big brown eyes at me and didn't budge.

In a training situation, I would have patiently coaxed him over with food and praise and a loving hand on his shoulder. It might or might not have worked. But this was real life, five o'clock in the morning, and I had had enough.

I wasn't going to try to make Cisco to cross that bridge. Not today.

"I'm going to take him around," I called across the creek.

"It only gets steeper downstream," Buck said.

"We'll be okay," I returned.

Famous last words.

Once we moved away from the bridge, Cisco was only too happy to pick up the pace. I pulled the line in closer and tried to keep up with him, which was a mistake. My flashlight bobbed erratically over the terrain that skirted the steep banks of the

creek, and just about the time I figured out that we could be in trouble, we were.

I said, "Easy, boy," as he negotiated his way around a big tree that grew at the edge of the bank. With his four paws and sharp claws, he had no problem managing the narrow ledge, but as I scrambled to keep up with him, my boot slipped across an icy rock and my feet went out from under me.

The flashlight flew from my hand and tumbled down the bank. I wasn't far behind it. I had the presence of mind to release my grip on Cisco's lead—proving that I was better trained than my dog—as I rolled and slid and bumped and sprawled down the twenty feet of ragged ravine. I felt my leg strike something, and an icy white pain stabbed at my knee. The cry I heard, I realized later, was my own.

I skidded to a facedown stop about ten feet from the water. It took me a long, dazed moment before I could even lift my head. When I did, I saw, to my amazement, that my flashlight was only a few feet away, still casting its steady beam through the tangled night. I could hear shouts above me, and the familiar sound of scrambling claws and panting breath. In another moment that hot breath was on my cheek as Cisco reached my side.

But by that time I hardly noticed. I had recovered my senses enough to see that the beam of the flashlight had caught something strange in its glow,

something familiar but weirdly out of place. I took advantage of that moment of numbness that precedes the onset of real pain to crawl to the light and pick up the flash. I held the beam as steady as I could, staring at what it revealed.

It was a shoe. A man's white running shoe, to be exact, and it was attached to a blue-jean-covered leg. The light was no longer steady as I moved it across the prone form: a hand, a shoulder, a neck. And a bloody mess where the face should have been.

I started to scream.

Chapter Four

I opened my eyes and a pair of muddy boots swam slowly into focus. The boots were crossed at the ankles, and they belonged to a pair of khaki-clad legs that were stretched out beside me. I mumbled, "Get your boots off my bed." My voice sounded thick and hoarse and my mouth felt like it was lined with cotton batting.

He said, "They aren't on the bed."

Strictly speaking, he was right. Only the ankles rested on Granny Applewaite's quilt; the boots themselves hung over the edge. But he sat up anyway and placed them on the floor, settling his shoulders on the pillow where his head had been a moment ago.

I would have liked to have berated him for that too, but I just didn't have the energy. Besides, for

five out of the past ten years, that pillow had been his. Strictly speaking, I suppose, it still was.

In 1995 I had had the very bad judgment to marry my high school sweetheart, voted the Most Eligible Bachelor of the class of '91 and Most Likely to Succeed, one Cecil Henry—Buck—Lawson. In 1998 I divorced him, only to marry him again eight months later. It took less than two years for me to discover that the only thing that had changed about him was that he had gotten better at hiding how bad he was at being married.

Unfortunately for both of us, the Most Eligible Bachelor of the class of '91 just couldn't seem to catch on to the fact that being married meant you couldn't be a bachelor anymore. Buck had an incurable weakness for other women. I had no sense of humor about it whatsoever. There had been three different women that I knew about—as I mentioned, he got slightly better at concealing his indiscretions the second time around—and after a while it wasn't even the cheating that got to me. It was the pure and simple embarrassment at my own gullibility. I refuse to allow anyone to ever make me feel that stupid again.

It's six years later, and Buck now lives in his mother's house, his mother having moved to Florida less than two weeks after he moved in—a decision with which I completely sympathize—and

I live in mine. We've found that we're both a lot happier that way.

I pushed my hair out of my eyes and looked groggily up at him. "What time is it?"

"A little after four." He glanced toward the window and added, "In the afternoon."

I groaned. I remembered the trip to the emergency room, the knee brace, the painkiller, and Buck carrying me up the stairs. After that, not much of anything . . . except the picture I couldn't get out of my head, of Luke Pickens with his face shot off.

I mumbled, "Are the dogs okay?"

"Yeah, Maude was here. She had to run into town to get your prescription filled, so I'm watching you."

I closed my eyes. "I'm not going anywhere."

"She left you some ginger ale." He picked up a glass from the bedside table.

I turned my head away. "I don't want it."

"You always were a rotten patient."

When I opened my eyes he was sipping my ginger ale through a straw. He looked almost as bad as I felt: face scruffy with beard, eyes puffy, hair mashed down into the unattractive waves and lines that come from wearing a hat all day. His lips were pale with fatigue and he still smelled like sweat and the cold, wild woods.

I said, "You haven't been here all day, have you?"

"No. I just stopped by to tell you"—his eyes met

mine and I focused sharply—"we found Cindy. She showed up at her mother's house about seven this morning, hysterical. She'd been pretty badly beat up, and she was shot in the arm. She's at Middle Mercy Hospital. They'll probably keep her overnight."

I tried to push myself into a sitting position, felt an immediate sharp throb in my knee for my effort and winced. "The little girl?" I said. "Angel?"

But before I'd finished speaking he was shaking his head. "Still missing. It's a hell of a story. Cindy says Luke had been drinking all day—probably on meth too, but she won't say it—and picked a fight with her about going out to get something to eat. He started beating on her, things got worse, he went out in his truck and brought back his .38, started threatening her with it, telling her to get Angel up out of bed and get in the truck. Well, somehow or another the gun went off and she ended up shot in the arm. Nothing serious—I guess the bullet went right through—but a lot of blood. Meantime, the kid is awake . . ."

I winced at this, at the ungodly picture it put in my mind, but he went on, "And she's kind of losing it, you know—Cindy, not the kid, although I guess both of them were really losing it by now—and the next thing she knows the two of them are being dragged into the truck. She figured he was taking her to the hospital, but he stopped the truck on the

highway, about four miles out of town, and pushed her out. He drove off with Angel. It took her five hours to get to her mother's house on foot. She was in really bad shape."

I stared at him. "She's a suspect in Luke's murder, right?"

He said, not looking at me, "She says she doesn't know anything after he pushed her out of the truck."

I stiffened my elbows and my shoulders, trying to pull away from him. It was a little difficult, given the softness of the bed and our proximity and the weakness of my muscles. I said, "Come on, Buck. The man who was beating up on her, the man who pulled a gun on her, the man who forced her little girl into his truck, is lying at the bottom of a ravine with his face blown off. Are you kidding me? She killed him; of course she did!"

He said simply, "Then where is Angel? If she killed him, why didn't she rescue her little girl? She's crazy with worry over her, Rainey. She loves that baby."

I didn't know how to respond to that. I was spared the necessity by the sound of a barking dog. I recognized the voice of Majesty, my ever-reliable watch collie, followed closely by Mischief and Magic, the Australian shepherds. Buck glanced toward the window. "I guess Maude is back."

He finished off my ginger ale, placed the glass on

the night table and sat up. "We've got about twenty people combing the woods now. Hank brought two search dog teams with him. Of course, it's kind of a mess right now, trying not to contaminate a crime scene." He glanced toward the window. "It's supposed to snow tonight."

I closed my eyes in silent frustration and helplessness. We both knew the twenty-four-hour rule, and in this kind of weather the chances that a missing child would live that long were even less. By tomorrow morning, they would be looking for a body, if they weren't already.

He stood and picked up his hat, which hung from the back of my mother's rocking chair. "We talked to Jim Peterson, by the way. He said he and a couple of buddies were out coon hunting last week. They used the cabin to get out of the wind and warm up. The trash and stuff were theirs. You need anything before I leave?"

"No." I sighed and added, "Thanks."

"I'm going home and get a few hours sleep. I'll let you know if anything turns up."

"Thanks," I said again.

At the door he looked back at me. "I'm sorry I got you into this, babe."

I tried to work my face into a scowl but couldn't entirely manage it. In the end I just sighed again. "Yeah, I know."

"I'll come by on my way into work tonight and let the dogs out."

"I can do it."

"No, you're supposed to stay off your leg. And you know you can't get up and down these stairs without help."

"Yeah, okay, thanks."

"I'll check on you later, then."

The thing was, sometimes he really could be a nice guy.

Maude Braselton had worked for my father for thirty-two years, first as his secretary when he had the law practice, and then as his clerk when he became a judge. With her crisp British accent and her exotic past, she added an air of glamour and intrigue to our little southern town, a role that she enjoyed immensely.

But to me, for all of our growing-up years, she was just Maude. I could not remember a Thanksgiving or a Christmas when Maude wasn't sitting at our table, and when I was nursing my mother through her last days of cancer, Maude never left my side. She was the one who made the phone calls, talked to the mortuary, and made certain that the casserole dishes were returned after the funeral. She was the one who went with me to pick out the casket when my father couldn't do anything but stare

out the window holding my mother's pink wool coat against his cheek.

Less than two years later, she was the one who went with me to pick out my father's casket.

Maude was the first person I ever knew who did something with her dogs besides hunt. She bred golden retrievers, and she trained them to do things that were, to me, as a young girl in an isolated mountain community, on par with what Seigfried and Roy did with white tigers. She gave me Cassidy, aka Summertime's Sundance Kid. For that alone, she would hold a place of highest honor in my heart for the rest of my life.

When I decided to open the boarding kennel and training facility, whom would I have approached about forming a partnership besides Maude? It was she who gave me all the support, advice and technical expertise that made it possible. Since retirement, she had downsized her own championship kennel to almost nothing, and she was glad to come in four or five days a week to help with whatever had to be done. She was my mentor, my business partner, my family. I don't know how I would have made it through the past few years without her.

After Buck left, she brought me a bowl of canned chicken soup and some hot tea, served on a tray with soda crackers and sliced cheddar cheese, just like my mother used to do. I felt guilty about letting her wait on me but knew she would be insulted if I

tried to stop her. Besides, all things considered, I deserved a little pampering.

"Cisco wants to see you," she told me as she unfolded the legs of the tray across my lap and fluffed the pillows behind my shoulders.

"I'm not speaking to him."

"Come on, now; you know it wasn't his fault. Not entirely."

I picked up my spoon. "Well, he'll never be another Cassidy, I'll tell you that." The minute the words were out I felt bad for saying them. After all, Cisco was as much her dog as Cassidy had been. I couldn't meet her eyes. I covered the awkward moment by quickly tasting the soup. "Thanks, this is great."

She lifted a napkin from a saucer at a corner of the tray. "Marge Peterson sent over this applesauce cake. Jim told her what happened."

I smothered a groan that was half delight and half yearning. Marge Peterson's applesauce cake was the best in the county, and it only had about twelve hundred calories a slice. "Take the rest of it home with you tonight." I thought better of that. "Okay, leave me half."

She pulled up the rocking chair and sat beside my bed, then proceeded to give me a report on business as normal while I ate, just as though I had not fallen down a cliff and landed practically on top of a murdered man less than twelve hours ago. That

was what I liked about Maude: she didn't let things rattle her.

"And a woman named Sonny Brightwell called," she concluded, after a recitation of everyday events so normal, so mundane, that I had been lulled into a comfortable daze, not really listening, just grateful for the sound of her voice. "Do you know her?"

I shook my head, trying to look as though I had been paying attention.

"I think she might be that woman who bought Earl Graves' place, out on Crying Rock. What did I hear about her? That she was going to turn it into some kind of retreat or commune or something."

A spurt of laughter almost caused me to choke on a forkful of applesauce cake. "That ought to go over real big around here."

Her eyes twinkled mildly. "You never know. The twenty-first century has knocked at our door, and sooner or later the world is going to find out where we live. Anyway she said she wanted to talk to you about a dog and would call back tomorrow. So." She placed her hands squarely on her jeaned knees and looked at me with a frank openness that invited confidence. "Tell me about it."

At sixty-four, Maude was still slim, athletic and vital. She had gorgeous platinum hair that was brushed back toward her nape in a sleek, no-nonsense fashion, and that flawlessly porcelain British skin. Her crystal blue eyes could convey

with a glance anything from hilarity to icy contempt, and when they were gentled with that easy compassion, as they were now, there was not a woman—or a man—alive who could resist spilling her heart out to her. So I did.

Luke Pickens was by all accounts a rotten kid, a worthless adult, a mean drunk, a dangerous character. When he was fifteen he and his older brother were both interested in the same girl. The two boys went out deer hunting one morning and only Luke came back. He told his daddy there'd been an accident, and sure enough, they found his older brother shot through the heart with a deer rifle. Luke was never brought to trial, although shortly after that his daddy, who was crazy about his oldest son, kicked Luke out and hadn't spoken to him since.

Some people felt sorry for Luke because of whom he had for a father. Some people just shrugged and said, "What could you expect?" Others speculate that had his mother, Ellen, who was actually a lovely woman by all accounts, and who came from a very good family, lived, everything might have been different. But she had died of cancer when her boys were still in elementary school.

I agree that Reese Pickens is one of the most disagreeable people I've ever met—not only mean, but slick about it, so that you never know how low-down he is until it's too late—and that it really is a shame to be thrown out of your daddy's house at

age fifteen. On the other hand, Luke never seemed to have much trouble making his way in the world, and certainly never seemed to lack the wherewithal for drugs and booze, and in my opinion if you wanted to keep your happy home you probably shouldn't go out and kill your brother.

I didn't like Luke, I didn't feel sorry for him and I guess like everybody else I was a little afraid of him. If I had heard on the radio what happened to him, I probably would have thought it was no better than he deserved, breathed a sigh of relief and gotten on with my day. But I hadn't heard about it on the radio. I had seen it with my own eyes, and I couldn't get on with my day. I wasn't sure that I would ever be able to get on with anything in exactly the same way again.

So it wasn't that I held any particular warmth in my heart for the likes of Luke Pickens, and I couldn't really say I was sorry he was dead. Maybe that's what made me so sad, and so angry, because by the time I finished I was sobbing like a baby.

Maude was a good friend, and she didn't have to say anything. She just sat there, holding my hand, and let me cry myself out.

Chapter Five

March in the mountains is a sly and treacherous beast: as sweet as a little girl in a white pinafore one day, and roaring down on you with bloody fangs and slashing claws the next. The ice storm of last week had given way to budding forsythia and yellow-headed jonquils that nodded gamely in the mud. From a nighttime low of thirty-four with a spattering of snow, the afternoon temperatures had blossomed into the sunny sixties. More snow was predicted by the weekend, and the temperature would plunge into the twenties.

I took off my sweatshirt as I leaned on my crutch, "helping" Maude to put Cisco through his paces on the dog walk. I was helping, instead of training, not because of my disability, but because Maude said I was in no mood to be handling dogs, and she was right.

Agility is a wonderful sport, a great training tool for almost anything you want to do with your dog. It builds confidence, speed, responsiveness, trust and, of course, agility. But most important, it cements a bond between human and dog that can be a thrill like no other.

Competitive agility trials have become one of the most popular dog sports in the world, and it is not unusual for a competitor to get up at the crack of dawn, drive two hundred miles, and wait at the trial site for seven or eight hours in order to get her chance at a forty-five-second run. Dogs are required to run an obstacle course that consists of jumps, weave poles, A-frames, pause tables and dog walks at top speed. This is not a problem for most athletic dogs.

The trick is that the dog has to take only the obstacles to which his handler directs him, and the handler herself does not know in which order the jumps and obstacles should be taken until she arrives at the trial. There is no practice. The handler memorizes the course, walks around it for a few minutes without the dog, and then hopes she can remember to give the right signals to her canine partner while running at top speed and trying not to trip over her dog or the equipment on the field.

If you succeed, you have what is called a "clean run"—you and your dog fly across the course in perfect unison, pivoting, turning, racing across the

finish line like poetry in motion—and it is a high like none you've ever known. If you don't succeed—well, that's why they call it a trial. Oh, and by the way, if you can't run the course in less than forty-five seconds, chances are that three border collies have already beaten your time.

All of my dogs train in agility, and during the spring and fall trial seasons we barely have a weekend free. Cassidy was, of course, a star. Cisco could be too, if it weren't for certain issues.

The dog walk, a bridgelike structure composed of two ramps and a cross board, was set to training level, barely three feet off the ground, and it had taken us most of the training session to get Cisco to even climb the up ramp. As I've mentioned, he has had some falls and it's not easy to rebuild a dog's confidence once he has had a bad experience. I shook my head in weary frustration.

"I can't believe I was crazy enough to take a dog into a rescue situation who can't even cross a bridge."

"I can't believe you tried to climb down a ravine in the middle of the night when you know you have a bum knee."

"Yeah, that, too." I sighed as Maude called Cisco, gave him a big treat and hug session, then tossed the ball for him. He raced across the muddy field with tail flying.

On any other day nothing could have dragged

my attention away from my beautiful dog and the pleasure it gave me simply to watch him do what a dog is supposed to do. But today the glint of sun on golden fur only led my eyes toward the mountains, and my thoughts toward the little girl who may or may not still be out there. *Damn it*, I thought, *I should be out there helping*. I couldn't believe I was stuck here, helpless, useless.

In the past twenty-four hours I had taken multiple calls from Hank Baker, Buck, Uncle Roe and even my buddies at the ranger station who had joined the volunteer search force. None of them had anything good to report, but still I carried the portable phone in my pocket, waiting for updates.

What were the chances that a six-year-old girl who was lost in the woods had survived the night, or would survive another one? And that was assuming that she had lived long enough to get lost in the woods, which was by no means a certainty. One thing we all knew, however, was that the longer she was missing the less likely it was that she would be found alive.

It was true that one more person wouldn't have made that much difference. If Hank and his dogs couldn't get a trail, what chance did I have? Still, I chafed to be out there doing something.

I gazed sourly from my knee, swollen and bulky in its brace beneath the leg of my sweatpants, to Cisco, who had just completed a perfect retrieve

and was sitting square in front of Maude, eyes brimming with eagerness, waiting for her to throw the ball again. What *had* I been thinking, letting Buck talk me into taking Cisco out? We both might have been killed.

My brooding thoughts were interrupted by a chorus of barks from the kennel and the porch of the house, where my other three dogs were confined. I turned to see a vehicle turning up the drive. I shaded my eyes but didn't recognize the white van, or its driver. When I cast a silent question toward Maude, who had also stopped to watch the van's approach, she shrugged. Given all that was going on, the sight of a stranger pulling up to the house was not necessarily a good thing, and I could feel my heart pick up the pace a little.

Maude released and praised Cisco and I called him to me as I hobbled toward the gate. "Come on, boy, let's go," I said and opened the gate. What I meant, of course, was that he should walk quietly with me to greet our visitor. What he thought I meant was that he should race the wind across the yard and fling himself joyfully on the driver's side door panel, barking and leaping for the window.

I shouted "Cisco!" and he didn't even look back. I didn't want to take a chance on giving commands I couldn't enforce, so all I could do was close the gate as quickly as possible and try to reach the vehicle before he did too much damage to the paint.

The driver was smiling and ruffling his fur as I got close enough to see, doing her best to encourage his bad behavior with affectionate comments like, "Yes, my dear, I understand. You're a wonderful dog, aren't you? It's such a pleasure to meet you!"

Now, I do appreciate someone who knows how to treat a dog, and especially when she does it with creativity and enthusiasm. And I am not one of those annoying dog trainers who scold other people for petting their dogs; I was raised to have better manners than that. But don't they realize that when you reward a dog with praise and petting for jumping up and clawing your car, you're just training him to do the same thing again?

"I'm sorry!" I called as I approached, stumping along as fast as I could. "He won't hurt you!" Not that she looked worried.

I got close enough to grab Cisco's collar, which I did, firmly. "Cisco, off!" I commanded, breathing hard. He dropped to a sit beside me, still panting and grinning at the newcomer, and didn't look in the least remorseful.

"I'm so sorry," the woman in the van said. "I didn't mean to make you run."

I grimaced and gestured with the crutch. "Not much chance of that." I was still breathing hard, but thanks to the two pain pills I'd downed before coming outside, no real harm appeared to have been done. "I hope he didn't hurt your car."

She laughed and gestured out the window to the side of her dinged and mud-splattered van. "Not much chance of that," she said, echoing me. She offered her hand, still smiling. "I'm Sonny Brightwell. I called yesterday."

"Raine Stockton." I shook the hand she offered, but it was a moment before I could put the name with the reason it sounded familiar. "Oh, right," I remembered. "Something about a dog."

She was one of those middle-aged tree-hugger types—I could tell at a glance—with a long braid of thick salt-and-pepper hair, no makeup, and pleasant lines of age and weather on her face. She wore a white fisherman's sweater that looked like an old favorite, and a faded pink Oxford shirt underneath. Natural fibers, no dyes or additives, vegetarian to the core. But she had a nice smile and seemed friendly enough; besides, a little tree hugging never hurt anyone.

She said, "I live over on the other side of Crying Rock. I bought sixty acres there last fall, and I'm just now settling in."

I nodded. "I heard you were going to build a spa or something."

She laughed. "Well, in a way, I guess. A spa for castoffs—that's not such a bad idea. Actually, I hope to eventually build a full-fledged animal sanctuary and working farm out there, but right now all I've got is a goat with an attitude, a rooster with a bro-

ken wing and a half dozen sheep. And that's why I'm here."

I was starting to like her, although I couldn't exactly say why. It might have been the rooster. "I don't know anything about sheep."

"Actually, I was hoping you might know something about sheepdogs."

She made a clicking sound with her tongue, and a small black-and-white head poked its way shyly under her arm, chin resting halfway on the window as though afraid of making a commitment. Cisco noticed immediately and started to lunge, but I caught him with a quick "Steady." He held on to his impulses with a great effort.

Sonny Brightwell said, "She showed up at my house yesterday morning, covered in mud and terrified. I got her cleaned up and fed and I could tell she wasn't a stray. Of course, under normal circumstances she would be welcome to stay with me as long as she likes, but there are the sheep."

I looked at her without comprehension.

"She chases them," Sonny explained, "to obsession. I'm afraid she's going to hurt one of them, or get hurt, and I can't keep her away from them."

I said, "Well, she's a border collie. That's what they do."

She sighed. "I know."

"I don't actually do much herding," I offered in a moment, trying not to remember the one disastrous

58

foray I had made into that sport with Majesty the collie several years ago—which was how, come to think of it, I had injured my knee in the first place. "But I know some people who do. If you don't mind driving a couple of hours, I'm sure I could arrange for lessons . . ."

Again she laughed. "Oh no, not me. I'm no athlete, and this little girl seems to think she knows all there is to know about herding sheep already. Anyway, I didn't come here looking for training. I was actually hoping you might be able to tell me where she belongs. I took her by the vet's yesterday, but he didn't recognize her. Said you might."

I offered the back of my hand to the black-and-white face in the window, murmuring, "Hello, sweet girl, aren't you a pretty thing?" while I thought about it. In fact the dog did look familiar, but I didn't want to rush things. And when she shied away from my touch, as though she had known the rough side of a human hand before, I was sure I didn't want to rush things.

I said, "There are a couple of people with border collies around here. I could make some calls, if you like. Maybe one of them will know something."

"Thank you." Sonny looked relieved. "I want to be really careful about where she goes, though. She's been through a lot already."

So. She had noticed the signs of abuse too. She rose another notch in my esteem.

She added, "In the meantime, though, I don't suppose you'd be willing to keep her? Just until her future is settled?"

I said, "Our boarding rate is ten dollars a day. Training and grooming are extra. Of course, if you want to turn her in as a rescue, there's no charge, but I'll give her to border collie rescue in Asheville after seven days of advertising for her owner. She won't stay here."

Sonny hesitated, and I tried to keep my expression pleasant and impassive. Then she said, "Maybe you could just board her to start with. If her owner doesn't turn up by the end of the week, well . . ." She looked at the dog, smiled and ran her hand affectionately through her ruff. "She's awfully bright, and I enjoy her company. Maybe we'll talk about some training."

I grinned my approval of her decision, not only because of the extra income it would mean for the business but also because my original opinion of her was validated. She was a dog person, and I had a feeling that one scared little black-and-white dog was about to find herself a good home.

Maude came up just then and I introduced the two. "We seem to have a runaway border collie," I explained. "Sonny can't keep her because she chases her sheep. We're going to be boarding her for a while."

Maude eased up to the window and had only

moderately better success than I had had in petting the dog. The closer a strange hand got to her, the deeper the little dog snuggled into Sonny's arm.

"You're welcome to walk her up to the kennel with me," Maude said. "That way you can get the whole tour and see that she's settled in."

Sonny glanced toward the kennels and shook her head. "I'm sure your facility is very nice, but maybe you'd better just take her."

She started to open the car door, and in one smooth move Maude whipped off the leather leash that was draped around her neck, looped it around the neck of the wriggling border collie and snapped it closed just before the dog plunged from the car, narrowly averting disaster. The dog lunged and dashed to the end of the leash in a 360-degree circle around Maude, who stood impassive and let her find her boundaries. Cisco watched the display with raised head and pricked ears but didn't dare break his down. Thank goodness.

Watching the frantic dashing and pawing of the air, I said, "How did you get her in the car?"

"Oh, she'll usually do what I ask her to . . . except where sheep are concerned, of course."

Maude said firmly, "That'll do, now," and gave a sharp short tug on the leash. Proving her sheep-herding ancestry, the border collie responded to the sound of a masterful voice and ceased her lunging. She crouched against Maude's ankle, trembling.

Maude knelt beside her with gentle praise and a handful of treats from her pocket, which the little dog sniffed politely but was too stressed to taste.

"I've tried to explain things to her from the sheep's point of view," Sonny said regretfully, "but she's been so traumatized it's impossible to reason with her."

I said wryly, "Yeah, I know the feeling. I try to explain my point of view to Cisco all the time, and he doesn't have the excuse of being traumatized."

She smiled as she closed the car door. "Maybe you ought to try seeing things from his point of view."

I lifted an eyebrow, and she nodded in an easy manner back toward the agility field. "For example, the reason he doesn't like crossing the plank is because he can't see where his feet are. He can't watch you and his feet at the same time. And he doesn't know what he's going to land on when he falls."

I lifted my eyebrows. "Do you do agility?"

"Goodness, no." She hesitated, looked down at Cisco and then looked back at me. "Pardon me. I don't usually just force my way into other people's affairs, but he did ask me to tell you that if you would stay about four feet away from him when he's up there it would be easier for him to see you, and he wouldn't be so nervous. But he still wishes he didn't have to walk the plank." She smiled apologetically. "That what he calls it."

"Oh," I managed after a moment, staring at her. "I see."

I was acutely aware of Maude straightening behind me with the little dog's leash firmly in hand, trying very hard to stay silent. Because I was a little afraid she might not succeed, I said quickly, "Uh . . . he told you that?"

Sonny looked at me for a moment, seeming to take my measure, and then smiled. "Don't be embarrassed. Most people don't understand what animal communication is all about. In fact, most people think I'm a nut."

I nodded gravely, biting down hard on the inside of my lip to keep from laughing. I murmured, "I'm sure that's . . . difficult for you." Damn. And she had seemed like such a nice person.

It's not that I don't believe in animal communication. After all, dog training is *all* about communication, and I communicate with animals every day—with my posture, my tone of voice, my face, my hands, my eyes and most important, hot dogs and cheese. And despite all this effort, I can assure you, not one animal has ever talked back.

Sonny Brightwell glanced down at Cisco and smiled. "He's a very talkative young fellow. He says he likes living here and you play lots of fun games together. He says he gets special food."

Well, okay. Like many golden retrievers, Cisco had developed food allergies, prompting me to put

him on a diet of fresh chicken organs, venison, and oatmeal. But anyone looking at that healthy, full-coated, bright-eyed young dog could guess he wasn't exactly fed on stale bread and water. Besides, wasn't all food special to a golden retriever?

"But today he's a little depressed," Sonny went on.

I heard Maude make a choked sound in her throat and I poked her in the ribs with my elbow. Sonny Brightwell was a client, and ten dollars a day was, well, ten dollars a day. However, I was starting to think I might be smart to ask for a deposit up front.

Sonny was gazing down at Cisco, who had settled on the ground with his head on his paws and his eyes half dozing. She said thoughtfully, "He's really sad about something he lost . . . a toy, a stuffed toy. It's in a hole. I think he buried it. Is that it, fellow? Did you bury it and forget where?"

Cisco did not favor her with a reply. Not a sigh, not a slap of the tail. He merely continued to doze in the sun with that air of single-minded contentment at which golden retrievers excel. I stole a glance at Maude, who was making less of an effort than I would have liked to keep her disdain under control. Her face, in fact, was twisted into such an unsightly grimace of amusement and contempt that I barely prevented a full-fledged guffaw of laughter. As it was, I couldn't stop a huge grin, and when I looked back at Sonny, she had, of course, noticed.

"I'm sorry, Miss Brightwell," I said, trying hard to sound sincere. I was probably less than convincing since I couldn't stop grinning. "I don't mean to hurt your feelings but—well, Cisco doesn't have any stuffed toys. The last one he had he eviscerated in twenty seconds flat. It took me days to pick up all the stuffing he'd scattered all over the house and yard."

Sonny did not seem the least offended. "Maybe that's what he's thinking of, then," she offered easily. "Still grieving for your poor shredded bunny, fellow?"

"Furthermore," said Maude with an icy dignity that would have made the Queen Mother shrink, "our dogs do not dig. Digging is a sign of a bored, intellectually understimulated dog, and we won't have it. None of these dogs has ever buried anything."

She made it sound as though Cisco had just been accused of burying Jimmy Hoffa, not a stuffed toy, and I suppose by her standards the crimes were about equal. Even Sonny seemed to get that, and when she looked back at me her eyes were twinkling.

"On the other hand," she said cheerfully, echoing my thoughts, "I could have made the whole thing up. After all, who's going to call me a liar? The dog?" She started the engine and passed a business card through the window. "Call me if you hear any-

thing. Take care of my girl, now." She smiled and waved. "It was nice meeting you, Raine. And you too, Cisco."

Upon hearing his name, Cisco got up, stretched and wagged his tail. She said to him, "You're welcome."

Then she winked at me and drove away.

I glanced down at the business card in my hand. SONORA J. BRIGHTWELL, ATTORNEY AT LAW. "Holy cow," I said and passed the card to Maude. Attorney at law? "Was she pulling my leg, or what?"

Maude's expression changed slowly from contemptuous annoyance to thoughtfulness as she looked from the card to the van that was disappearing around the curve of the drive. "*Now* I know who she is," she said with only the slightest measure of surprise.

The border collie started to lunge again and barked once, sharply, after the car. If Miss Sonny Brightwell was such a smart animal communicator, I wondered why she hadn't picked up on how distressing it was for the poor little dog to be abandoned here by someone she had, apparently, just begun to trust.

"She's a nut," I volunteered, holding on to Cisco. He waved his tale happily as I dug into my pocket for some crispy hot-dog treats. Sautéing, or microwaving for five minutes, sliced hot dogs brings all the fat and flavor to the surface and makes an almost irresistible treat for dogs. Most dogs, anyway.

The border collie had absolutely no trouble resisting my offered treat, her eyes focused fixedly on the place where she had last seen the van.

"Better put this little girl in an enclosed run," I added, straightening up with the untouched hot-dog slice still in my hand. An enclosed kennel was chain link embedded in concrete, roofed and surrounded by another chain-link-enclosed run. I had seen dogs less agile and less motivated than this one, when under stress, escape from the regular ten-foot-tall chain-link runs, and with her runaway history I was taking no chances.

Maude shrugged and passed the card back to me. "I don't suppose you have to have all your crackers to get into law school."

"I've known a few lawyers who are proof of that."

"Sonny Brightwell." Maude pronounced the name with a ruminative frown. "I knew I'd heard the name before. She's some kind of environmental lawyer from the coast. She handled that big lawsuit some years ago over the waste treatment plant on one of the Barrier Islands. Won it too. I think I heard something about her representing a Save the Mountains group up here."

"Good for her." I asked Cisco to sit, then tossed him the treat. "You know what else she is?"

Maude nodded. "A nut."

We grinned at each other as we started back to-

ward the kennels, Cisco trotting happily alongside and the little border collie in tow. But the encounter had left a vague uneasiness in the pit of my stomach that stayed there the rest of the day. And I couldn't stop thinking that somewhere in the middle of Sonny Brightwell's crazed ramblings there was something important, something that ought to have made a connection with me.

If only I hadn't taken so long to figure out what it was.

Chapter Six

Day three. The sky was misting snow that melted in mud puddles and congealed on car tops. In the mountains in the winter, the sun often doesn't clear the horizon line before nine a.m., and today it looked as though dawn might not make it here before sunset.

Hank Baker sat at my kitchen table, digging into a good-sized stack of pancakes spiced up with blueberries that I'd frozen from last year's crop. I thought it was the least I could do. The big country kitchen was warm and cheery with the glass doors open on the fire in the wood-burning stove, the smell of bacon in the air and the happy sound of barking dogs occasionally wafting in from outside. William and Rufus, Hank's bloodhounds, were on the screen porch chowing down, and Majesty the

collie made a nice foot warmer underneath the table.

We talked about Alice, Hank's wife, and his boy Henry who was going off to college this fall. We talked about who was new in tracking class and who was planning a litter of puppies for the spring and about the article in *Front and Finish* on last fall's field trials in South Carolina. What we did not talk about, for the longest time, was the search.

It was day three, and Hank was going home. From now on, regardless of all hope to the contrary and in spite of what the police did or did not admit in public, they would be looking for a body.

So despite the reflected flames dancing in the glass doors of the woodstove, despite my mother's colorful scatter rugs on heart pine floors and artificial light bouncing off buttercup-colored walls and copper pots, despite the smell of blueberries and bacon and the feel of warm collie fur beneath my feet, the gray heart of winter invaded my kitchen and seeped into every corner, and nothing I could do would make it go away.

At length Hank pushed back from his empty plate with a satisfied sound, and I refilled his cup from the coffeepot in the center of the table. "Good spread, Miss Rainey, mighty good. That ought to get me most of the way down the road. I appreciate it."

"Little enough," I said. I mopped up the last bit

of syrup on my plate with the corner of a by-now-cold pancake. "I sure wasn't much use where it mattered."

Hank leaned back in his chair, cupping his hands around the mug of coffee. His face sagged with fatigue and sported a three-day growth of ash-colored stubble, not a good look on a man whose most distinguishing characteristic on his best day was the three carefully preserved strands of snow-white hair that were draped across his bald head like ribbons around a balloon. He gazed morosely into the coffee cup.

"What I just can't figure out," he said, "is why we didn't pick up a trace. I mean, if she was out there, and if she was moving, there's gonna be scent. We had enough good dogs out there that we should have picked up something. So I keep thinking . . . I don't know. Maybe she never was in the woods. Maybe he let her go on the road somewhere, just like he did her mama. Maybe whoever shot him took her."

I was silent. We both knew there was a much more likely scenario, and it was that she *was* in the woods somewhere, but she wasn't moving. Maybe she never had been.

"It was a tough grid to cover," I offered after a moment. "And we contaminated a lot of it the first night, what with Cisco taking off like a crazed thing and cops trampling all over everything."

He sipped his coffee, and I sipped mine.

I added, as casually as I could, "So, I don't suppose you went back and checked the shed where Cisco made his 'big find' "—here I made quotation marks in the air with my fingers—"did you?"

He shrugged. "The police had already cleared it. No point in wasting manpower."

"Nothing in the area? Not even an almost?"

He looked at me curiously. "We had close to three hundred acres to cover. We didn't go back over anything that had already been searched. How come?"

I actually opened my mouth to reply but spared myself the embarrassment just in time. You don't ask someone else to validate your mistakes. I shrugged instead and hedged, "You know how it is. You hate to give up."

He sighed heavily. "Don't I know it."

Hank put his coffee cup on the table and pushed back his chair. "Well, I thank you again, but I guess I'd better get on the road before the snow gets any worse."

"They say it's going to clear up."

I got my crutch under my arm and walked him to the back door. Majesty crawled out from under the table, yawned and stretched and sniffed the air in hopeful anticipation of breakfast leftovers.

Hank eyed my stiff knee meaningfully. "You

know you're going to have to have that thing operated on."

I grimaced. "It's not that bad."

"If it was one of your dogs, you would've had it fixed two years ago."

He had me there. "I'll just be more careful."

He looked at me for the liar I was. "See you in class next month?"

"I'll try."

He opened the door onto the screen porch, where his two hounds, having finished their breakfast, were waiting contentedly. He gave them each a scratch behind the ears and glanced back at me. "You've got a good dog in that golden. He's just young, that's all. I'd hate to see you give up on him."

I smiled without conviction. "Maybe. Do you need any help with the dogs?"

"No, get on back inside before you freeze. I'll talk to you in a few days."

"Drive carefully, Hank. And . . . thanks. For coming up."

He nodded. "You mark my words," he said, and I could not be entirely sure whether the firmness in his tone was an effort to convince me or himself. "If that little girl was ever out there, she was buried long before we let the first dog loose."

I swallowed hard, tasting the bitter remnants of coffee on the back of my tongue. *Buried.*

There it was again, that stirring of uneasiness, that niggling little suspicion of something over-looked, something I should have thought about. Only this time, I thought I knew what it was.

It was stupid. A crazy idea. But to tell the truth, I almost lifted my arm to call Hank back. I didn't. There were a lot of reasons, but the main one was, quite simply, that I didn't want to be wrong again.

Or I didn't want to be embarrassed again.

A chorus of muffled barks from the kennel ac-companied his departure, and through the window I watched him drive away as I dialed a number on the cordless phone. Buck got off work at seven a.m., spent a leisurely hour over breakfast at Miss Meg's downtown, and usually got home around eight thirty. I knew he was on schedule today because I had seen his car turn into his drive while I was tak-ing the last of the pancakes off the stove.

Over hill and dale, so to speak, Buck and I live al-most five miles apart. But if you could string a cable from my house to his, I could swing down it and be on his front porch in one minute flat. The peculiar-ity of mountain terrain is such that, even though my property is relatively flat and doesn't appear to be on a particularly high elevation, it is some fifteen hundred feet above the main highway. And in the wintertime, before the leaves bud out on the trees, I can see every twist and turn of three county roads and the state highway, including the long, winding

dirt drive that leads to my almost-ex-husband's house. This can sometimes be convenient.

He answered on the third ring. Unfortunately, I don't have a view of his actual house, much less his windows, so I couldn't tell whether he had already gone to bed or was just getting out of the shower. I hoped, because he was so cavalier about interrupting my sleep, that it was the former.

"Hey," he said when he recognized my voice. He sounded tired but awake. "What's up?"

"That's what I was going to ask you."

He sighed. "You know what I know, sweetie. The damn news trucks have been camped out at the office since yesterday. Looks like a satellite transfer station downtown."

"Bet Uncle Roe loves that."

"He does have a little bit of the ham in him."

"I saw Cindy's mother on TV yesterday. I felt so sorry for her. I wondered why Cindy didn't make the appeal herself."

"She was still in the hospital."

"Yeah, but you'd think under the circumstances they'd let the cameras in. I'm sure Cindy would've wanted it."

He was silent. We never did very well when discussing Cindy Winston, so I moved on.

"Hank was just here. He's on his way home."

"Yeah. We pulled two deputies off the search too."

That only confirmed what I already knew. You didn't deploy valuable manpower on a search that was unlikely to turn up a live victim. The weight of the unspoken acknowledgment was heavy between us.

Then I said, "I want to ask you something."

He answered cautiously, "Shoot."

"Do you know a woman by the name of Sonny Brightwell?"

"Yeah, I know her." He sounded relieved that this was a question he could answer. "At least I know of her. Middle-aged gal, from Savannah, I think. A lawyer. She made a bundle seeking justice for the little guy, so the story goes, and retired up here. Bought the old buffalo farm on Crying Rock. Her daddy was in real estate, seems like. Divorced, no children. Plans to run the place by herself. Stayed through the winter, so maybe she will. Pete Calvin said she put in a whole new kitchen and ordered solar panels for the roof. One of those tree-hugger types, I guess. How come?"

Not for a moment did I doubt that I had asked the right person. There's something about Buck and the opposite sex. Women trust him, confide in him, rely on him. He's the one they call in the middle of the night when a tree limb lands on the roof, or on Christmas Eve when the heat goes out, or on Monday morning when their car won't start. And it's not just the young, pretty ones, either, although they do

admittedly seem to be in the majority. Old ladies and pigtailed girls find him just as charming as do barroom waitresses and buxom divorcees, and in all fairness to Buck, he is just as solicitous of the six-year-old who needs help untangling her shoelaces as he is of the twenty-six-year-old in tight shorts and a halter top who needs help changing a tire. Buck is one of those rare men who is genuinely interested in women. He listens to them because he wants to; he knows what they need and he gives it almost instinctively. Women, therefore, young and old, pretty and plain, flock to him like metal shavings to a magnet, and it really isn't his fault. It's just the way he is.

What *is* his fault, of course, is how he responds to the women once they flock to him. And that's why we live apart.

Moreover, in this case, as in so many others, he didn't even have to meet the woman to know all about her. Again, that was just the way he was.

I answered, "I met her yesterday. She brought a dog in."

"So?" He took a bite out of something, and the word was muffled.

"Do you think she's on the up and up?"

"She'd better be. She just got hired to represent that citizens' action group—who are they? Friends of the Mountains? Anyway, she's doing it pro bono—I think they retained her for a dollar—but

they've got a lot riding on it. They're having a big meeting down at the community center Friday, and that was all anybody could talk about until—well, until this other. Don't you ever read the paper?"

"So you think she's okay. I mean, no record or anything?"

"Well, I didn't run a check on her, if that's what you mean. What's the matter, didn't she pay her kennel bill?"

"No, nothing like that. I was just curious about her."

He waited for me to say something else. I wanted to say something else, a lot of somethings. I wanted to tell him my suspicions about the border collie, even though they probably didn't mean anything. I wanted to ask his opinion on this crazy little theory of mine, and I didn't really want to hear it. I wanted to see whether he could spare a few hours this afternoon to check it out . . . and I didn't want to be wrong. Especially in front of Buck.

He couldn't entirely keep the edge of impatience out of his voice when he said, "Did you really call just to do a credit check on your new boarder? Was there anything else?"

Things used to be so much easier between us. My only problem was that I kept forgetting that.

"No," I said. "I just wanted to see if you'd heard anything. About the case, I mean."

"You know you'd be the first."

"Yeah, I know. Well, I won't keep you. Get some rest."

"Yeah, I'm beat. Two double shifts in a row. Listen, Raine . . ." His voice was quiet now, and serious. "You did your best, okay? Try not to get too wrapped up in this one because, well . . . it doesn't look like it's going to have a good ending."

I took a deep breath and let it out slowly. "Yeah, I know. Bye, Buck."

I stood thoughtfully holding the phone for a moment after we'd hung up. The snow was a light mist that did not appear to be sticking to much, but the day was still ugly and foreboding—perfect for staying inside by the fire, using my injured knee as an excuse to curl up with the dogs and catch up on all my back issues of *Clean Run*. Instead, I grabbed my jacket and paused only long enough to give Majesty a quick stroke on the head. "Stay away from the table," I told her and left the dirty dishes sitting there as she sighed and stretched out on the rug in front of the stove.

Maude had the *Today* show on in the office and a black-and-white dog standing calmly on the grooming table while she brushed out its coat. I did a double take before I recognized the border collie that Sonny Brightwell had brought in yesterday.

"Holy cow," I said, closing the door softly behind me. "She sure calmed down."

"Pretty amazing," Maude agreed. "I guess Miss

Animal Psychic must have finally gotten through to her."

I reached into my pocket for a piece of cheese and offered it open-handed to the little girl. She nibbled it delicately, a vast improvement over yesterday, when she was too stressed to even eat.

I said, "You know who she belongs to, don't you?"

Maude met my eyes. "I do."

By mutual unspoken agreement, we let the subject drop. She turned her attention to a stubborn mat behind the border collie's left ear, and I said, "Where's Cisco?"

"I put him out in number three with Missy and Magic. Do you want to work on his weave poles today?"

The number three she referred to was our covered outdoor run, where we exercised the dogs on hot, wet or snowy days like today. A lot of people might think a covered outdoor run was an unnecessary expense, but believe me, when you have twenty dogs who've been penned up in six-foot kennels all weekend and it's been raining for three days solid, it's worth every penny.

I said, as casually as I could manage, "No, I think I'll give him the day off. I was going to ride over to Marge Peterson's and return her cake plate. Thought I'd take him with me."

"I'll do that, on my way home tonight."

"That's okay."

We both paused as the national news gave way to local headlines. Our cable service was out of Asheville, eighty-five miles away, so it was unreasonable to expect everything that happened in our little county to be covered on television. The exception was, of course, a kidnapping, a murder and a missing child.

"Still no word today on missing Angel Winston, who was abducted from her Hansonville, North Carolina, home early Tuesday morning. Her kidnapper was later found shot to death in a wooded area of Hanover County, but there was no sign of the missing six-year-old. Sheriff Richard Bleckley states that no arrest has yet been made in the shooting, and that the department's full resources have been dedicated to finding the missing child."

Throughout the segment a photograph of the blond-haired girl was broadcast in a corner of the screen. It might have been a school photo: her face was a little more lean and her hair a little longer than in the Santa dog picture, and she was wearing a dress with a big collar. Her expression was just as grave, her lips just as determinedly unsmiling, as they had been when her arms were around a big golden dog in a Santa hat.

Damn it, I thought, and the stab of helplessness and anger felt like a physical blow in the pit of my stomach. *Damn it*.

We were silent until the local weather forecast was finished—precipitation ending by noon, high forty degrees, which meant it would probably snow all day and never rise above freezing—and then I said, "Well, I'm going to go on over to the Petersons' before the snow gets too high." I started toward the kennel run to get Cisco.

"Hold on a minute and I'll go with you. You shouldn't be driving."

"No, I'm fine. I drive with the other leg. I'll probably run on into town while I'm out. Do you need anything?"

She looked at me for a moment, knowing full well I was up to something but lacking the evidence to prove it. Then she slipped a loop leash over the border collie's head, lifted her to the floor and said, "Drive carefully. And take your cell phone."

"Will do." And I hurried out before she could say anything else.

The dogs were playing a lively game of tag when I came up, but they all charged the gate, leaping and pawing, when they saw me. A lot of people would have severely criticized my training practices for allowing that kind of behavior, and I would have placidly ignored them. To tell the truth, I kind of like being the center of someone's universe—much less three magnificent creatures like the ones who fought for my attention now. And there is an awful lot to be said for having a dog who thinks that you

are even more exciting than someone of his own species.

So I spent a few moments playing a little game with them, giving commands like "sit," "down" and "shake," and tossing a cookie to the first dog to comply. They loved that game and were quickly vying with one another to be the first to do as I asked. At the end of the game, I opened the gate and released Cisco out into the corridor and rewarded the other two with dog biscuits.

I went toward the exit with Cisco in heel, but then, on impulse, pushed open the door of the training room as I passed. Cisco followed me in with a great deal less enthusiasm than he had shown in the exercise run.

It was cold inside, and the only light came from the big windows at either end of the room and from the skylight overhead. I didn't bother switching on the fluorescents; I didn't plan to be there that long.

I took Cisco to the end of the dog walk and told him to stay. He did so, ears down and tail wagging lowly. I hobbled around to the other side of the bridgelike structure and placed a piece of cheese at the bottom of the down ramp. I returned to the middle ramp of the dogwalk and then carefully stepped about four feet away from it.

I said, "Cisco, walk it!"

Cisco went quickly up the ramp and then, without hesitation, scampered across and down. When I

reached him he was happily licking cheese off his whiskers, front paws on the floor and back paws on the ramp, just as he had been trained to do. His ears were up and his tail was waving.

I grunted skeptically and took him back around. This time I kept my usual position close to the dog-walk. He got to the top ramp and assumed his customary position, belly low, barely slinking across. When I tried it again, this time standing well away from the equipment so he could see me, he sailed across.

"Well," I muttered, frowning a little, "what do you know about that?"

Not that I gave any credit to Sonny Brightwell, of course. It only made sense that Cisco would feel more comfortable when he could see where I was, and I would have figured that out without her help sooner or later. Still, it was interesting.

"Come on, boy," I said when he paused at the end of the dog walk, looking at me expectantly. "We're done for the day. Let's go for a ride."

Cisco waited in the truck while I struggled up Marge Peterson's front steps with the cake plate, hoping that if I fell and broke something, it wouldn't be the plate. Fortunately, Marge saw me from the window and came rushing out to help with a sweater held over her head. She made a big fuss over my being out on crutches and I apolo-

gized for not calling first, and when we were settled all cozy in her front room I thanked her for the cake and told her how much I had enjoyed it, and she brought coffee, which I drank.

Eventually the conversation turned to what was on everyone's mind, and what was, in fact, the reason for my visit. "Can you believe this awful business?" She sighed, her eyes turning to the wooded view beyond her window. "I know the good Lord says to love our neighbors, but nobody ever deserved killing more than Luke Pickens. As for that Winston girl, well, I wouldn't believe a word that came out of her mouth if she had one hand on the Bible and the other on her mother's grave, but nobody deserves to lose a child like that. Nobody."

"We don't know that she's dead," I said, a little sharply.

Marge Peterson looked at me sympathetically. "Well, I don't see how she couldn't be, do you?" Then she leaned in a little closer, a look of something like dread speculation in her eyes, and said conspiratorially, "You don't suppose she did it herself, do you? The mother, I mean. Like that crazy girl in South Carolina that drove her babies into the lake and told the police they were kidnapped?"

I shivered at the thought. I couldn't help it. The possibility was too plausible, and the story too close to home, and the world we live in too crazy not to

allow room for all explanations. I said, "I don't know." And I added fervently, "I hope not."

"You know she went home yesterday."

"Who? Cindy Winston?"

Marge nodded. "Elsie Dickerson, who works over at the hospital—she told me. You know what else she said?"

I lifted my eyebrows in question.

"She said the doctor didn't even want to keep her overnight, that she wasn't nearly as badly hurt as she made out, and that gunshot wound she supposedly had? Didn't even need stitches. Barely a scratch." She sat back in satisfaction.

"Then why did they?"

"Why did they what?" She sipped her coffee.

"If she wasn't hurt bad enough to keep overnight, why did they?"

"Oh, well, my dear. The *police* asked them to. That's what I heard. Do you know anything about it?"

Many people still make the mistake of assuming that, because of my former relationship with a sheriff's deputy, I am privy to inside information about anything and everything that has to do with law enforcement in this part of the state. Well, considering the rather ambiguous nature of my relationship with the sheriff's deputy in question, I supposed some confusion was understandable. But people

had even asked me to fix speeding tickets for them, and that was just plain weird.

I shook my head. "I didn't even know she was out of the hospital." Marge looked disappointed, compelling me to add, "You have to feel sorry for her, though. Being stuck in the hospital while her little girl is missing, lost in the mountains, and she can't even get out and help search."

Marge nodded gravely. "Unless . . ." She left the sentence unfinished and I wondered why Hank hadn't mentioned seeing the child's mother at search headquarters yesterday. If she had been released from the hospital, surely that was the first place she would have gone. Unless . . .

I put my coffee cup down on the table nearest me. It rattled delicately against its saucer. "Marge," I said, "do you think Jim would mind if I took the shortcut across your back pasture to get home?"

She looked confused, as well she might. "It's awfully muddy," she said uncertainly.

"I've got four-wheel drive. To tell the truth, there were some places we searched the other night that I wanted to have a better look at in the daylight, and it would be easier to take the logging road than to go around."

"Well, I guess it would be all right. But if you want to wait a bit and let Jim go with you, I'm sure he'll be home in a minute. He just ran over to the le-

gion hall to see about getting the heat turned on for the bingo game tonight."

"No, thanks." The last thing I wanted was someone else to watch me make a fool of myself—again. "Just don't let him shoot me if he comes back and sees me poking around in your woods," I joked and pushed myself to my feet.

"Well, you be careful out there. Here you are with a broken leg . . ."

I didn't correct her misapprehension. Sometimes appearing harmless is a good thing. "Don't you worry. I might let my dog out to run, if that's okay. Thanks again for the cake. You take care, now, you hear?"

By this time I had my coat on and was out the door, hoping that, once I had gotten what I wanted, I hadn't appeared to end our visit too abruptly.

The reason I did not choose to drive back to Three Mile Creek Bridge and hike in the way we had come Tuesday morning should have been obvious: Hiking, with my knee in a brace, was pretty much out of the question. Moreover, if I went that way I was bound to run in to someone in an official capacity and that, for reasons that were slightly less obvious, was the last thing I wanted to do.

It might have been just as easy to pick up the logging road where it opened out onto Old Hapeville Road about three miles from my house, but it's just

a matter of good manners—not to mention good sense—to let a person know when you're about to go trespassing on his property. Maybe I should have let Hank know my plan, or Maude, or even Uncle Roe, but there was no way I was ready to do that. It's not that I mind making a fool of myself that much, but I *hate* making a fool of my dog, particularly twice in a row.

All of this subterfuge, deception and effort was, believe it or not, because of one little word. The first time I had heard it, it had been easy to ignore because it had been uttered by a woman who was eccentric at best, crazy at worst, and because I had been too busy laughing to listen to the proddings of my subconscious. The second time the word had been used in an entirely different context, by someone I knew and trusted. For whatever reason, it had set off the same jingling of bells—not quite alarm bells, but definitely "pay attention" bells. And what I started to pay attention to was a suspicion that was too obvious—or maybe just too wild—to be ignored.

The word was "buried."

The road was muddy and badly rutted, littered with fallen tree branches and almost impassable in places. By the time I pulled the truck off the road and put it in park, my knee was throbbing. Cisco sat beside me in the front seat, secured by his canine seat belt, and as soon as we stopped he began pant-

ing and looking around alertly, almost as though he recognized where we were.

"Okay, boy," I murmured, "no pressure. We're just going to have a look around." I slipped my cell phone and a flashlight into my parka pocket, snapped on Cisco's leash and got out of the car.

The snow had left only a light dusting on the ground here in the woods, but the leaves were slippery, and I used a sturdy branch in one hand and Cisco's lead in the other for balance as I made my way the fifty or so yards into the woods. Cisco was sniffing the ground in an eager crisscross pattern, but that didn't mean anything. Dozens of footprints, animal and human, had no doubt left their scent on this trail since Tuesday morning.

Likewise, the area around the shed had been so trampled, rained on, snowed on, frozen, thawed and snowed on again in the past three days that nothing in the way of footprints or scent would offer much information about who had been here. Besides, it wasn't scent evidence that I was looking for.

Here's the thing: Cisco *had* alerted. He had been inside the shed and none of us could see what he had found, but he *had* given that one short bark from a sitting position that had never, since he had begun training, meant anything except he had found what he was looking for. By the time we arrived and Buck and Wyn had done their big-city-

cop-secure-the-perimeter routine, Cisco had been distracted by the baked beans and I had been humiliated. But what if we had gotten there a moment sooner? What would we have seen?

It's in a hole.

I edged my way through the sagging shed doorway with Cisco on a tight leash. There were so many holes in the walls and the roof that snow-brightened daylight made the flashlight unnecessary. I stood just inside the doorway for a moment, looking around, getting my bearings.

There was a pile of old tractor equipment in the corner, and the remains of an ancient Hoosier dusted with snow. On a shelf sat some fruit jars that had probably, at one time or another, been used to hold moonshine. A length of rotted rope on a nail, a moth-eaten mule collar, a hammer with a broken handle, the detritus of a hundred years of farm life. On the crumbling remains of the rock hearth was the charred circle of a campfire littered with partially consumed cigarette packs and candy wrappers; the scene of Cisco's big find.

I picked my way carefully across the floor, acutely aware of the clinking whisper of snow on the metal roof, the panting of my dog, the scrape of my own footfalls—the only sounds in a place that was suddenly far too quiet, far too empty. I leaned down and gave Cisco a reassuring pat—reassuring for me, not for him—and that was when I saw it.

On the northern wall, not far from the fireplace, was a spot that had been cleared of leaves and debris. A casual observer might have simply thought that the wind had blown the spot clear. The casual observer would not have been looking for, nor would he have noticed, claw marks in the dirt, which, upon closer examination, revealed what was not a dirt floor at all, but a slab of wood. And even though this was what I had come here to find, when I saw it my throat went tight and my pulse started to race.

I dropped Cisco's lead and he went straight to the spot, sniffing it with avid interest, and then— just as he must have done the other night—digging experimentally at the edges of the concealed door.

How could Buck have forgotten about the root cellar and the trapdoor that led to it? How could I? Every kid in the county had played here at one time or another, had made a hideout or a fortress out of it, had locked his little brother inside, had concealed childhood treasures in its depths. Every one of us had thought he or she was the *only* one who knew about it.

I don't remember stumbling across the room and dropping to the floor—I was that scared, that hopeful, that terrified of what I would find. My throat was so dry and my breath so heavy that I felt as though I was drowning as I frantically felt around the edges of the door, found the worn metal hook

that once had supported a rawhide loop and lifted the door upward on its hinges. Cisco backed up, surprised yet curious, as the smell of cold earth rose up to meet us.

I fumbled in my pocket for my flashlight, and the beam shook noticeably as I shone it inside. In the old days, this subterranean room had been used to store root vegetables and preserves through the winter, to shelter the family from severe storms and—who knows?—maybe even to hide them from enemy attack. There were sturdy steps carved deep into the earth, and though my recollection from childhood was that it was a cavernous place, fully big enough to hold a dragon and a sea serpent or two, there were in fact only six steps leading downward, and the entire chamber couldn't have been more than six by eight feet. It was, as my wildly erratic light slowly revealed, empty.

Or at least it was empty of human forms, and that was all I cared about at the moment. I stretched out on my stomach over the opening so that I could sweep the interior with my light, and I was just about to draw in my first full breath since I'd spotted the trapdoor when my flashlight beam brushed over something. And the breath caught in my throat.

Actually there were two things. The first one was lying crumpled against the bottom step, obscured by the angle of the wall so that it was only partially

visible to me. It had gleaming, sightless eyes and pale, thin hair.

It was a child's stuffed toy.

Had it not been for the knee brace, I probably would have scrambled down the steps and snatched up the artifact, although I'd like to think that at least some of the past ten years of being married to a policeman, not to mention being raised by a judge, would have rubbed off and I would have remembered, even if at the last minute, the rules of evidence. As it was I remained frozen in place, gasping for breath, holding the flashlight in both hands until the slamming of my heart subsided to a mere roar in my ears. Then I slowly, and none too steadily, moved the beam in a searching arc toward the other object that had caught my eye. And I didn't breathe at all.

Finally I wiggled back from the opening, sat up and put my arms around my dog. "I'm sorry, Cisco," I whispered. "You were right. I'm sorry, boy. Good boy, good dog."

Cisco licked my face.

I took a deep breath, struggled to my feet and pulled my cell phone from my pocket. I dialed 911.

Because the other thing I had seen in the cellar was the metallic gleam of a gun.

Chapter Seven

Uncle Roe looked at the bagged toy one more time before handing it over to one of the deputies. His expression was, as usual, phlegmatic. "Well, just talked to the grandma. She says it sounds like a doll Angel slept with. Said she never went to bed without it. She's on her way to the office now so we can get a positive ID. But it sure doesn't look to me like this thing has been here more than a couple of days."

"Me either," I said, shivering. Now that the excitement was over, I guess a little shock was setting in. I could feel it in my throbbing knee and in the biting cold I hadn't noticed so much before. "I mean, I know kids play here all the time—at least we did when we were kids—but when I saw it I just knew . . ." I let the thought trail off, because there

really was no good conclusion for it. "What about the gun?"

He stuffed his gloved hands into his parka pockets and turned his back to the wind. "We already called in the registration, should have that later today. But we'll have to send it down to the state crime lab for a ballistics match. That could take a few weeks."

"I mean fingerprints," I said impatiently. "Can't you get fingerprints and, like, find out who shot it?"

I heard one of the deputies snicker behind me and I turned to glare at him. It was Cal Hodgkins, whose dad used to go hunting with my dad, who had been four grades ahead of me in school and who had been cocky back then too. He said, "Too much TV, Rainey." And then one of the other guys called him away before I could shoot back a retort. I was too tired to think of one, anyway.

I turned back to Uncle Roe and he just shrugged. "He's right. Never that easy in real life."

I felt my frustration mounting. After all this, I had expected the gun to be the clue that solved the case—even if it couldn't lead us to the missing Angel. "But if that's the gun that killed Luke, why wouldn't fingerprints tell you who did it?"

"Maybe they will." His tone was as mild as ever. "On the other hand . . ." He took his hands out of his pockets and held them up. They were swathed in insulated gloves, just like mine were. "It was

awful cold that night. If the shooter was wearing gloves, no fingerprints."

"Why leave the gun there?" I wondered, my mind leaping from one subject to the other like a nervous dog guarding a stash of bones. "Why leave it with the doll?"

"Stashing evidence, maybe. Most likely meant to come back for it, but you got here first. Or maybe"—and though there was nothing particularly ominous or accusatory in the next words, though in fact his tone did not change at all, the words chilled me to the bone—"he was just in a hurry to get out, and dropped both items without realizing it."

And then he looked at me more intently. "What made you come back here, anyway? And how come you didn't remember the root cellar the other night?"

I swallowed hard and evaded his gaze. "You knew about the cellar just as well as I did. None of us was thinking very smart that night." My eyes landed on the Explorer, where Cisco was curled up in the back, probably fast asleep, and I corrected myself silently, *Most of us weren't thinking smart*.

Then I looked back at Uncle Roe, frowning a little. "What do you mean, you talked to the grandmother? Why didn't you talk to Cindy? I thought she was out of the hospital."

"She is. She's staying with her mother until . . .

well, until. But her mother didn't know where she was when we called."

What kind of mother didn't stay by the phone when her child was missing?

I said bluntly, "Do you think she killed Luke, Uncle Roe?"

His eyes revealed absolutely nothing, and neither did his tone as he replied, "Now, sugar, you know it don't make a damn what I think."

"But do you?"

"We don't have any suspects right now."

I hated it when the cops in my family started talking like cops to me. Next he'd be telling me to run along home like a good little girl, but first I had to ask one more thing. My voice was low and a little hoarse as I said it. "Uncle Roe, do you think she was here the other night—Angel, I mean, in the cellar, while we were searching? And that's how the gun got there, and the doll, because someone was holding her captive, and she was there all the time?"

He just looked at me, and he said, "Maybe. But you'd know that better than I would. After all, it was your dog that found the place."

I felt hollow inside.

The area had been secured with crime scene tape, the evidence had been collected, the guards had been posted, and there was nothing more to be done here. Uncle Roe gave me a bracing squeeze on the

shoulder that was also meant as a dismissal, and he said, "Good work, Rainbow. You get on home now and take care of that knee. We'll let you know what we come up with."

In other words, he couldn't leave until I left. So I hobbled back to the car, and I left.

Sonny Brightwell's house was reached via a winding, one-lane dirt road that climbed halfway up Crying Rock Mountain, turned in on itself, and slid halfway down the other side. The only signs that someone did indeed live at the end of the trail were occasional hand-painted NO HUNTING signs and the gravel spills that filled in the worst of the potholes. There was a falling-down log-pole barn, a brand-new chicken coop with a slanted metal roof and lots of cross-fencing, some of which had been recently repaired, but much of which was still in shambles.

The log house, the cross-fencing and the pole barn had all been built in the seventies by a retired doctor who moved up here to raise buffalo. Apparently the market for buffalo meat was not what he expected, and the cost of retirement—even on the side of a mountain in the middle of nowhere—more than he'd anticipated, because he then turned his hand toward manufacturing controlled substances in the basement of his log home.

There he would be today had he not had the ex-

traordinary bad fortune to purchase a piece of
equipment for his private pharmaceutical enterprise that was too big to fit through the basement
door. He called a contractor to enlarge the door,
who called his brother to give him a hand, who
was—more bad luck for the doctor—an underpaid
sheriff's deputy who just happened to be picking
up some extra work on the side. The deputy en-
larged the door, because that was what he was
being paid to do, helped the doctor move the equipment into his illegal lab and returned three hours
later with a warrant for his arrest. True story. It was
my father who sent the doctor to state prison, where
he died three years later of a stroke, I think.

At any rate, it was a nice piece of property with
lots of level grazing land, and the leftover fencing—
courtesy of the buffalo—was an added bonus. No
doubt the price had been right too, because in the
past thirty years the only other buyers had been a
lesbian couple who tried to start an underground
newspaper—they lasted two years—and a retired
husband and wife from Minnesota who had
planned to turn it into a bed-and-breakfast. I'm not
sure they even cleared escrow.

By the time I made my way out of the woods and
up Crying Rock Mountain, it was close to two
o'clock. Fortunately the snow had stopped and the
temperature had in fact risen above freezing, or I
probably wouldn't have made the trip. I've got to

admit, my knee was killing me, and the four ibuprofen I had taken didn't even take the edge off the pain.

So what was I doing here when I should have been at home with my Percocet and my ice packs and my elevated footrest? I didn't have a good answer for that. It had something to do with the way I'd mumbled and avoided Uncle Roe's eyes when he asked me what had made me come back out and search the cabin. It had a lot to do with the way he had looked me straight in the eye and said, "You'd know that better than I would. After all, it was your dog . . ."

Maybe the killer had used the place to stash the doll and the gun, trying to hide the evidence. Maybe Angel had never been there at all. And even if she had, no one could be sure that Angel was still alive when she dropped the toy, which had turned out to be a floppy-limbed soft doll with fuzzy white hair, exactly the kind of thing a child might take to bed with her and refuse to relinquish when she was awakened and swept from her house in the middle of the night. Of course, the presence of the gun certainly suggested that the kidnapper, whoever he was, had been there with her. There was no way of telling when, or for how long.

But what if Angel *had* been in the cellar that night when Cisco alerted? What if she had been at the bottom of the stairs with a hard, angry hand over

her mouth so she couldn't scream and a gun pointed to her little head while we roamed about upstairs, making jokes and kicking aside debris with our boots? What if she had been there, listening, praying, believing in the way that little girls should always believe that the good guys had come to save her, and then listening as we walked away?

That was the possibility I could hardly bear to think about.

Embarrassment, pride, and skepticism had already caused me to make one potentially fatal mistake. So I guess that was why I was here.

I pulled up close to the house, where, I was happy to notice, someone had installed a wheelchair ramp. I hated trying to negotiate stairs with crutches and usually ended up only pretending to use them, which of course defeated the purpose of having crutches in the first place.

I gathered up the awkward implements from the front seat and opened the car door. "Stay here," I told Cisco. "I won't be long."

Cisco glanced up from his blanket on the bench seat, yawned elaborately, and lowered his head again. Except for potty breaks, he had been in the car for almost five hours today. I vowed silently to make it up to him somehow as I planted the crutches on the ground and eased my way out of the truck.

"Oh, no," called a cheerful voice to my left. "Let him come with you. Everyone is welcome here!"

An open door, a friendly voice and an unqualified welcome were all it took to make my obedience-trained dog forget his "stay" command and come over the seat and out the door as though shot from a rocket launcher—well, that, and an orange and white cat that streaked across my path almost the minute Sonny had finished speaking.

Cisco sprang from the front seat and over my head with a litheness that would have earned him cheers on any agility course in the country, and hit the ground with paws scrambling. I screamed, "Cisco!" but he apparently thought I was cheering him on. The orange cat tore across a stone-lined flower bed—which fortunately was empty at this time of year—with Cisco in hot pursuit. Skidding across the floorboards of the front porch, leaving long, mud-streaked pawprints in his wake, Cisco overturned a wicker table and bounced off a concrete plant stand, then sailed off the porch into a mud puddle that was big enough to swallow a Volkswagen. He splashed out of the puddle at top speed, slid on a patch of ice and rolled. He was on his feet without missing a beat, sprinting like a gymnast after the cat, who was by now perched in the cradle of an apple tree, looking down on us all and laughing.

And so, I was relieved to see, was Sonny Bright-

well. That was the first thing that surprised me. The second was that she was in a wheelchair.

"Oh, my God, what I wouldn't give for a camera!" she exclaimed, wiping her eyes with the back of her sleeve and still gasping with laughter. "That dog needs to be in the circus."

"I am so sorry," I managed, cheeks flaming. I fumbled in the car for a leash and commanded sternly, "Cisco, come!" praying a desperate little prayer that he actually would.

I needn't have worried. The game was over and Cisco sat at the base of the tree with his tongue lolling, looking and no doubt feeling rather foolish. Since he had nothing better to do, he turned and trotted toward me.

I snapped the leash on his collar and repeated, "I'm so sorry. I wish I could say he's usually better behaved but . . . not really. He's a golden retriever," I added, as though that explained everything.

She waved a dismissing hand, and I was glad to see that her eyes were still dancing with amusement. "It was Hannibal's fault. He likes to tease the other animals. He had Cisco in his sights before you even opened the door. Come on inside; we'll get him cleaned up."

I protested that Cisco was far too muddy, that we had done enough damage, that I'd just lock him in the car, but she was insistent. I followed her up the ramp with a happily complacent Cisco at my side,

righting overturned furniture and plants as I went, and before I knew it we were in a stone-floored mudroom, working together with old towels and a bucket of soapy water to scrub the mud off Cisco's paws and coat.

Really, there's nothing like bathing a dog to break the ice, and Sonny was so good-natured about the whole thing that even I could laugh about it by the time we were done. "Cisco is not my best advertisement as a dog trainer," I admitted wryly and rubbed the last smear of mud off his nose. "I keep hoping age will improve him."

"Well, I guess we all could stand some improving, couldn't we, young fellow?" She tossed a towel into a nearby hamper and declared, "Well, you look presentable to me. Why don't we go in the house and sit down? I put on a pot of coffee before I went out in the yard, and I might even be able to scare up a little something for our canine friend, here. If, of course"—she tilted her head up at me—"it's okay with you."

I emptied the bucket of muddy water into the utility sink and mopped up as best I could. "Thanks, I think our canine friend has put you to enough trouble. But a cup of coffee sounds great."

I felt surprisingly comfortable as I followed her into the big country kitchen, Cisco now in a perfect heel at my side. I generally find log homes dark and depressing; too much wood and not enough win-

dows for me. But the convict doctor had spared no expense on his retreat. He had carved a big bay window into one wall and cut generous skylights in the roof. There was a pass-through fireplace that was really big enough to pass through, and the bed of embers that had formed beneath the low-burning flames of two big logs gave off a radiant heat that could be felt midway across the kitchen. The floor was covered in flagstone, and the countertops were granite—although I could tell that this last was a recent addition. The kitchen had obviously undergone some remodeling to make it more handicapped accessible: the upper cabinets had been replaced with below-the-counter ones; the countertops themselves, along with the sink and cooktop, had all been lowered. The refrigerator was one of those sliding-drawer kinds that I had only seen before on televised home shows, and I gave an appreciative, "Wow," as she opened it to take out the cream.

She grinned at me. "Pretty cool, huh? Just because you decide to go back to nature doesn't mean you can't enjoy all the advantages of a technological world, I always say. Sugar?"

"No, thanks. This place is really great."

"Would you like to see the rest of it? I'll take the coffee into the living room."

She placed a tray with the coffee cups and a plate of cookies across the arms of her chair, and she managed it all so smoothly that it never even oc-

curred to me to offer to help. I followed her through the oversized rooms, noting that the big wheels on the electric chair were designed for a smooth ride over the stone floors, and that the sparse placement of furniture provided for easy access. The decor was vaguely Scandinavian, with splashes of red and azure in the artwork and upholstered furniture, and all the windows left uncurtained to take advantage of the light and the spectacular views. It was nothing like I expected, and Sonny laughed as I told her the story of the doctor, the buffalo and the ill-fated drug enterprise.

We settled in the living room, on the other side of the pass-through fireplace, and I said, "You've really done a great job with this place. It must have been a lot of work."

"Thanks. I debated for a long time about whether to try to build over the floors with something that's a little easier to get around on. I'm glad I didn't."

"They're beautiful," I agreed. I dropped into a wing chair with a firm seat and sturdy back, and propped my crutches up against the side of the oversized hearth. "It would be a shame to cover them."

I said, "Cisco, down," and he stretched out beside my chair. He really does have very good house manners, once he settles down.

Sonny had placed the coffee tray on an ottoman between us, and she spent a few moments pouring,

stirring, offering cookies. I saw that her movements were careful and just a little stiff as she handed me my mug.

"I noticed the animals on my way in," I commented. "You've got quite a collection. Are you really going to start a sanctuary?"

"Eventually. Right now I just take what comes my way. The rooster I found on the side of the road. I guess he'd been hit by a car. A neighbor was going to shoot the goat. And the sheep I got from Lionel Perkins in Cantwell. He was auctioning off a whole flock—I think he said he'd just bought it from somebody around here. But the old and the sick ones nobody was going to buy were about to be killed, so I had him deliver them over here."

We talked about animals for a while, easy talk with which we were both comfortable. I sipped my coffee, keeping one eye on Cisco and the other on the cookie plate until he finally dropped his head to his paws and closed his eyes. Good house manners could go out the window in an instant when cookie plates were placed at dog-nose level.

After a moment, because my curiosity wouldn't let me be silent a moment longer, I said, "I didn't realize you were . . ." I searched for the right word, the way people always do. Disabled? Handicapped? Physically challenged? "That you used a wheelchair."

"I don't always," she replied. She bit into a

cookie and made an appreciative sound. "Are you sure you won't have one? They're not homemade, but they're good."

I reached for a cookie, and Cisco looked up. I glared at him. He closed his eyes again.

Sonny said, "I've had rheumatoid arthritis since I was thirty. It's genetic. Some days are better than others, but to be safe I use the chair as much as possible. I'm a long way from help if I should fall."

Her casual courage in the face of what was, in fact, a life-altering disease made my own injury and the inconvenience it entailed seem petty. I said, because it was the first thing that came to me, "Did you ever think about getting a service dog?"

She hesitated with the cookie poised before her lips, as though the thought had never occurred to her before. "I suppose I should," she agreed, "eventually. But to tell the truth, I never thought about it."

"When you're ready," I urged, "we should talk. I can recommend some fine agencies."

She smiled. "I will. Thanks." Then she said, "Thank you for coming, but when I left the message, I really didn't mean for you to drive all the way out here."

I must have looked blank, because she prompted, "I called this morning. I talked to—oh, dear, I can't remember her name, but I'm sure I said you should call me, not come out."

I shook my head a little to clear it, trying not to think of all that had happened since the last time I talked to Maude. "Sorry, I didn't check my messages. It must have been Maude you talked to. She's in charge of the kennel when I'm not there, and most of the time when I am." I gave a feeble little grin and at her questioning look added, "I came to see you about . . ." Well, about what? This was going to be harder than I had thought. "Something else," I finished lamely.

"Well, isn't that a coincidence?" She smiled, inviting me to continue, but I quickly grasped the chance for evasion.

"You first," I said. "What did you call about?"

She looked a little wry as she glanced down at her coffee cup, which she held with both hands. "Actually, and I don't want to make a big deal about this, but what I called about was to tell you . . ." She sighed and put down her cup with a slight rattle. "I felt badly after I left the dog with you yesterday. I know I should have said something then but"—her glance had a note of entreaty in it that I found thoroughly confusing—"I was afraid you wouldn't take her if you knew. A lot of people won't."

I said, "If I knew what?"

"That she bites," Sonny confessed. She added quickly, "Not habitually. At least I don't think so. And she's never bitten me."

Then how, I wondered, could she know the dog

bites? But before I could ask that question—which, in retrospect, was a rather stupid one—Sonny answered it for me.

"But I would hate it if someone got hurt because I didn't say something, so I felt I should let you know. It seems she ran away—or got thrown out, or abandoned; it's not clear—after biting someone. It was during a thunderstorm, I think, or some kind of loud noise, and she was frightened and well . . ." She shrugged and opened her palms. "That's what I know. The dog's side of it, anyway."

I didn't point out that there hadn't been a thunderstorm since August, nor did I inquire as to exactly how a dog might tell her side of the story, whatever it might be. All I said, in fact, was, "A lot of border collies are noise sensitive. Have you ever seen her snap, or snarl threateningly?"

Her reluctance was obvious as she admitted, "She was frightened when I first found her, and she did growl and snap and try to look as vicious as she could. But she calmed down as soon as she realized I was there to help her."

I nodded. "That's not unusual behavior. I'd have to spend a lot more time with her before I could give you a real temperament evaluation, of course. Biting is never a good thing, but sometimes there are extenuating circumstances."

She looked relieved. "Oh, I'm so glad you feel that way. I just didn't want her to start out with one

strike against her already. So, how is she? Any luck tracking down the owner?"

I dodged that question without much grace. "It's a little early to expect anyone to be looking for her yet. But she's doing great. Much calmer today."

Sonny sat back in her chair and sipped her coffee with careful, deliberate movements. "Oh, good, I was hoping so. I asked Cisco to talk to her, to tell her that she was safe and in a good place. Sometimes they're more likely to listen to one of their own species. Thank you, Cisco." She smiled at my dog, who sighed in his sleep but made no other sign of acknowledgment, and then she glanced back at me, her eyes twinkling. "You still don't believe me, do you?"

And so. There was no time like the present. I took a breath. I looked her straight in the eye. I said, "The other day, when you were talking to Cisco"—that was hard to say—"you said something about a bunny. A bunny that was buried and that he couldn't find. What made you say that?"

Her eyes were guileless, interested but puzzled. "I'm sorry, I don't remember the conversation exactly. I think you told me that your dogs don't bury things."

"Maude told you that," I replied impatiently. "It's true, but what I want to know is what made you say 'bunny' specifically. What made you say 'buried'?"

Her brows knit over her smile, reminding me of an earnest, intelligent collie who wants to please but just doesn't understand. "I really don't know. I said bunny because that's what Cisco was looking for, I guess. A fuzzy pink bunny that was buried in a hole."

I felt blood leave my face and pool in my extremities. My fingers tingled. My toes felt numb. My knee throbbed.

Sonny's expression changed quickly to concern. "Are you all right? You're white as a sheet."

"Look." My voice was sterner, and louder, than I meant it to be, mostly to keep it from shaking. My fingers tightened around the coffee cup until I could feel the strain in my shoulders. I tried to gentle my tone as I repeated, "Look. I like you, I really do. But a little girl's life is at stake and no one has time for games. I need to know what you know and I need to know it now."

"Oh, dear." She sat back with a breath, her eyes dark and big. "That's what this is about."

"Angel Winston dropped a pink bunny slipper when she disappeared," I said with sudden anger. "That's what we gave Cisco to get the scent. How did you know that?"

Now it was her turn to lose color. "Oh, my God." She didn't blink, or breathe, or even move, but as she stared at me she seemed to shrink into herself, to grow smaller as I watched.

"Oh, my God," she said again, and for a long time she said nothing else. She just stared at me with a kind of stunned disbelief, as though waiting for me to unsay the words.

Then she drew in a breath that stuttered in the middle, and she leaned forward to set down her coffee cup. The movement was jerky and she almost missed the table. I moved quickly to steady the cup before it clattered to the floor, but coffee sloshed over onto the stones. She didn't seem to notice.

She said in an odd, hollow voice, "I didn't. I didn't know anything. Not about the bunny slipper, not about anything." Another breath, but it did nothing to strengthen her voice. "It *is* a game, don't you see; that's exactly what it is. I just—make things up, whatever comes into my head, and when I get it right people say, 'Oh, my God, you're psychic!' and when I get it wrong people still say, 'That's exactly what Rover would say if he could talk!' because that's what they want to *believe*. It's just for fun; it's never really *mattered* before."

I felt oddly disappointed as I said, "So you can't really talk to animals?"

"I don't know," she answered slowly. "How would I know? How can I know whether the things I'm getting are coming from the animals or my own imagination? Like with the border collie, for instance. I saw her snap and snarl at me when she was cornered, and it's not such an illogical leap to as-

sume that she's bitten someone before, and maybe that's why she's homeless. My imagination could be just filling in details, even though it seems to me at the time that the thoughts are coming directly from the animals . . . . But *this*." She shook her head, partly in frustration and partly in amazement. "I've never had to deal with anything like this before."

She hesitated, and a pinched expression of trepidation narrowed the corners of her eyes. "Did he find it? The slipper?"

I shook my head impatiently. "He wasn't looking for the slipper. He was looking for the child. The slipper was just a scent article."

Sonny looked at Cisco. "He thought he was looking for the slipper. And I think he found it." She raised her eyes to me and corrected, boldly, "He says he found it."

"Well, he didn't. What he found was—" And I stopped, cut off in mid-thought by the truth. I looked at Cisco. "What he found was," I finished more softly, "the place where we think the little girl was held hostage."

"And if she only dropped one slipper," concluded Sonny Brightwell, "she was presumably still wearing the other one. So he did find it."

And we both looked at Cisco in silence for a moment. Cisco, never one to turn down an opportunity to be the center of attention, returned my gaze with

eager expectation. And I stopped pretending I didn't know why I had come here.

I said quietly, "Does Cisco know where she is now?"

Sonny was silent. I couldn't even look at her. I just kept my eyes focused on Cisco's alert, deep brown ones and I wished harder than I had ever wished anything before that I really *could* talk to him.

"No," Sonny said at last, her voice heavy with regret. "I'm sorry. He doesn't understand what you want."

As she spoke, Cisco dropped his head to his paws and heaved a great, golden sigh. It was almost too perfect.

Sonny said, in a voice that was gentle and still laced with regret, "Please understand. I know you don't believe me. I'm not sure how much of it I believe myself, although I think I believe more right now than I did before you came in. I can only tell you what I think. Cisco says he wants to make you happy. He tries very hard. He just doesn't know what to do. He says he's sorry he's not like the other one."

I looked up at her sharply. "What other one?"

"The one you loved best." Her face was implacable, her eyes on Cisco. "He says he tries to be like her because he knows you miss her. He wants you

to know that he would have gone in her place if he could have. But he couldn't. And he's sorry."

I looked at her for a very long time, saying nothing, thinking nothing, refusing, to the best of my ability, to even feel. At last I put my coffee cup down, somehow got my crutches together and struggled to my feet. I said, "I've taken up too much of your time."

Sonny made some kind of protest, but I don't know what. There was puzzlement and a little hurt in her face. I didn't care.

"I have to go." I looked around for my coat and told Cisco to heel.

"I'm sorry I couldn't be of more help," she said.

I said something. I hope it was polite.

She went with me to the door and watched from her chair as we got into the car. I think she waved. I just wanted to go home, and I didn't look back.

Chapter Eight

"All in all," Maude remarked three hours later, "I would say you've had quite a remarkable day."

I was wrapped in a quilt on the sofa with a cup of brandied cocoa, a stack of photo albums and four dogs for company, trying to lose my worries in a trip down memory lane. It wasn't working.

I said morosely, "And I can't believe I just spent most of it talking to a pet psychic."

"Well, that part was fairly lump-headed," she admitted, dropping down onto the sofa beside me. "Did you learn anything?"

I had to take a sip of cocoa before answering. "Nothing I didn't already know." I turned my attention studiously to the photo album, and Maude knew, of course, that there was something I wasn't saying.

But in typical Maude fashion, she didn't press

me for information I wasn't ready to give. "I tried calling Buck," she said. "Just curious if he'd heard anything about who the gun belonged to."

"He wouldn't know anything; this is his day off."

"He knows everything. Unfortunately, he's not answering his phone."

I glanced at the clock. It was suppertime, dark outside, and Buck was more of a TV dinner-and-beer kind of a guy than one who was likely to run into town for dinner—not that there were that many options for dinner even if he had been. Even when we had been living together, it was hard to talk him into driving the thirty-five miles to the nearest movie theater or decent restaurant. When he had a day off, he liked to stay at home. Unless, of course, he had a date.

Which, of course, was none of my business.

Maude glanced at the photo album on my lap and smiled. "My, she was beautiful, wasn't she? Gorgeous head."

There were three females in the wedding photo to which she referred: the bride, who happened to be me, the mother of the bride, and the flower girl, a golden retriever. I had absolutely no trouble figuring out to which of us she referred, and it wasn't just the remark about the head.

The photos were from the first time I had married Buck, and another person might have wondered what romantic notions had inspired this

sentimental journey. I looked young and hopeful in my floaty white dress and flower-wreathed hair, my mother so vivacious and sunlit that it was hard to believe that anyone with that much zest for life could ever depart this world. Even Buck looked good minus ten years and twenty pounds. But that wasn't the reason I kept this album and pulled it out from time to time to run my fingers lovingly over the pages, as if by touching the images I could somehow magically touch the spirit they represented.

Cassidy was in almost every picture, all decked out in a wreath of blue and white flowers, holding a beribboned basket filled with ivory roses. Buck's hand rested lovingly on her head. My father posed with her on the church steps. Mother and I stood smiling down at her. Anyone would have thought it was *her* wedding. In fact, as usual, she had been the star of the show.

Maude and I flipped pages silently for awhile, smiling now and then at a particularly compelling snapshot, pointing out a detail, occasionally giving voice to a wistful murmur. We went through a couple of albums in this way, and when I opened the next one the only photographs there were of a fuzzy blond puppy.

After I found out about Buck's last indiscretion, there had been no big fight, no tearful recriminations, just a sad, quiet good-bye. He had come in

one night and seen the truth in my eyes, and I had seen the guilt in his. He packed up his things and moved out without a scene.

A couple of months later, Buck had shown up on my doorstep with a fuzzy blond puppy in a box. I had only to look at the pup to know he was Cassidy's grandson. The only one of her offspring who was still producing litters was in Ohio. How Buck had discovered that, and what he had gone through to get me a puppy, I couldn't begin to imagine.

He had said, "I know it's not the same, and I know it won't make everything all right. But I thought at least this little guy could keep you warm at night, and maybe, when he grows up, keep an eye on you for me."

I had loved him so much at that moment—and hated him so much for making me love him—that to this day I don't know how I had the strength of character to keep from flinging myself into his arms and begging him to move back in again.

"Well," I said and closed the album. The subject of the puppy photos, who was napping on the rug in front of the fire, rolled over on his back, paws in the air, head stretched out flat against the floor. It's hard not to chuckle when a dog does that, but I couldn't even manage a smile. Maude noticed, of course.

"Well, indeed," she said. She stacked up the photo albums and returned them to the shelf under

the coffee table where they belonged. "Always lovely to visit old times, isn't it? So helpful in putting things in perspective."

I said softly, "She said Cisco thinks I loved Cassidy best. And that he knows he'll never be good enough for me."

"Sometimes it's helpful to give a voice to those who can't speak for themselves," commented Maude. "Sometimes it's not."

"Do you think he—"

"Oh, don't be absurd. And even if he did, he wouldn't care. Why do people persist in investing their dogs with emotions that only humans—thank God—are capable of possessing? Look at him, for heaven's sake."

I looked at Cisco, who had found a rubber Kong toy and was patiently examining it for any remnants of the peanut butter with which I sometimes stuffed the toy to make it more enticing. He nosed the toy along the floor, pounced on it, and carried it back to the rug before the fire, where he lay down, took the Kong between his paws, and began to chew. Maude was right, of course. Dogs view the world and everything in it only in relation to how they affect them. They couldn't care less what privileges others might acquire as long as they themselves don't feel deprived. How I envied him, at that moment, a dog's ability to live almost completely in the present.

I said, "She knew about the bunny slipper."

"She most certainly did not. I was there that day, remember? I heard every word. She talked about a buried toy and called it a bunny, but you just got through telling me that even *she* was surprised when you told her about the find."

"I never would have gone back there if what she said hadn't stuck in my mind. Maybe if I hadn't been so skeptical, I would have gone back sooner."

"And it wouldn't have made an iota of difference."

I lifted my cocoa cup, found only dregs and set it aside with a sigh. "God, I feel like such a failure."

Maude swung her booted feet onto the coffee table, attracting the attention of Magic, one of the Aussies, who came to have her ears scratched. This, of course, incited the jealousy of Mischief, her sister, who bounded over, tailless butt wagging, and tried to wiggle her way into the center of the action. They were both young dogs and should have been crated before now, but they had been so good that I'd allowed them to stay up past their bedtime, so to speak. That all ended approximately twenty seconds after the first one tried to leap on the sofa and steal a kiss. In a master stroke of efficiency that was poetry in motion, Maude sent each to her crate with a Nylabone and a cheery word, snapped the doors shut, and returned to the sofa, leaving both of the

dogs happily thinking that bedtime had been their idea. She really is my hero.

"I once knew a girl," said Maude as she settled down again, having elicited no more than a bored yawn from Majesty and an alert look from Cisco, "—now you'll find this interesting—I once knew a girl who within the space of three short years lost her mother, her father, her husband, her job and her best friend. Can you fancy it?"

"Hmm," I said tonelessly. "Dreadful."

"Oh, it was, it was. But what was odd about this girl, unbelievable, really, is that somehow through the process, instead of taking the whole thing as just a series of life's blows, unjust as they often are, she decided that it was somehow all her fault. Moreover—and this is the fantastic part—she determined that it was within her power never to lose anything again. She about drove herself batty, trying to make sure of it."

She fell silent, and her face, in profile to me, was relaxed and contemplative. She would have waited forever. I was half-inclined to let her.

Finally, I asked, grudgingly, and without any warmth whatsoever, "Okay. What happened to her?"

"Oh, it was quite impossible, of course," Maude replied cheerfully. "You can't control everything. You can't win every time——not in agility, not in obedience, not in search and rescue. You can't be re-

sponsible for things that are out of your control, like life and death. Sadly, my poor friend didn't realize this until it was too late. She ended up knitting cozies for kittens in a home for the hopelessly insane."

I said, blank-faced, "Kittens."

"Oh, indeed."

"I don't knit, Maude."

She smiled. "Shall I teach you?"

I met her gaze dead-on. "This is not about winning. You know that. There isn't a blue ribbon at the finish line. If I fail this time, I'm not the one who loses."

"You haven't failed," she returned acerbically. "Neither has your dog, which I certainly hope is apparent by now."

I said quietly, "Cisco did his job that night. If I had done mine, if I had looked where he told me to, Angel Winston would be safe at home right now."

"You don't know that. There's no proof that she was there while you were searching the building the first time, and even if she was, the most likely scenario is that you would have lifted up that trapdoor and been shot, or she would have. And how conveniently you've rewritten history to make it appear as though you were the only one there. If I recall, two sheriff's deputies, a half dozen other search teams and the high sheriff himself made the same mistake you did."

"That doesn't make it any less of a mistake."

"It also doesn't make it all your fault, now, does it? How disappointing that must be to someone who could save the whole world if only she had enough hours in the day."

I grimaced, not quite willing to give her the smile she wanted, but knowing better than to engage in a full-blown debate with Maude when she got on her high horse like this. Besides, she was probably more right than wrong. I didn't like to fail, and I did take failure personally. But in this case, I just didn't see anything wrong with that.

Abruptly, Cisco abandoned his toy and stood up, his head swiveling toward the door and his hackles raised. He gave a soft, uncertain growl. At the same moment Majesty came rushing in from the kitchen, toenails scrabbling on the hardwood floors, barking her shrill collie bark.

I said, "Majesty, quiet!"

Maude said, "What in heaven's name?" She started to stand.

And then the world blew up.

Chapter Nine

"Why would anybody do this?" I sat shivering on the front steps, one arm around Cisco and the other around Majesty. The night was a cacophony of barking dogs, crackling radios and whirling lights. Fire hoses were stretched across my front lawn, every floodlight on the place was glaring, and two police cars were angled haphazardly across my mother's peony bed. To their credit, both dogs were sufficiently impressed by the gravity of the situation to resist their instincts to go bounding happily from police officer to firefighter, and stayed close by my side.

"Tell me again what you saw," said Uncle Roe, who looked more tired than I could ever recall. His eyes were dark-circled and his normally round features were beginning to sag, and I felt bad about bringing him out here, despite how scared I was.

"Nothing. I didn't see anything." Another con-

vulsive shiver racked me and I buried my face in Majesty's warm coat, breathing in heated air. "We were just sitting there, and—"

"And the dogs started barking," said Maude, draping a blanket over my shoulders. I already wore my coat, but the shivering came from the inside. "I thought I saw headlights reflected in the windowpane, as though someone was turning to pull into the driveway, and then there was a flash and an explosion. What was it, a Molotov cocktail?"

"Looks like it."

The bomb, whatever it had been, had landed in the yard well short of the house, and the fire had been more show than substance. It had burned itself out long before the volunteer fire department had arrived. But it had come awfully close to the kennel, and the dogs inside were still barking mayhem.

I sat up straight in alarm. "The border collie," I said. "Sonny said she was noise sensitive. She could jump the fence—"

"She's fine," Maude assured me with a brisk pat on my shoulder. "I just checked. They're all fine."

"They're not fine," I shot back angrily. "They're scared to death! They could have been killed! What if Majesty had run out the dog door instead of into the living room? What if Cisco had?" Again I shuddered and I must have unconsciously squeezed the dogs harder than I had intended because Majesty wriggled away. Cisco licked my face. "What kind of

maniac would do something like this? I've got innocent dogs here!"

Roe said gently, "I don't think they were trying to hurt the dogs, sugar. I really don't even think they were trying to hurt you. A Coke bottle full of gasoline and a short fuse is not exactly the kind of weapon you use if you're trying to do somebody in."

"Well, what the hell do you think they were trying to do? Pay me a compliment?" I could feel tears burning my throat and my eyes and I hated the taste of them. I scraped them away with the back of my sleeve.

He shoved his hands into the front pockets of his coat and looked far less worried than I thought the situation merited. "Warn you, probably. It's the kind of thing some good old boy would do to make a point."

"A point about what?" Maude wanted to know.

"Good question. Let me ask you something else. What do you know about somebody called"—he glanced down at his notepad, squinting a little in the strobing lights—"Brightwell. Sonny Brightwell."

I swiveled my head around to stare at Maude, who in turn raised her eyebrows in surprise. Roe missed neither gesture.

"You know her?"

"She brought a dog in to board with us," I said.

"A runaway, actually," Maude pointed out.

"Not necessarily." I felt oddly protective of the

little border collie. "Maybe a stray. Anyway, she's paying the kennel bill, so it's none of our business where the dog came from."

"That's it? That's all you had to do with her?"

I shrugged uncomfortably. "Well, I did drive up there to see her this afternoon."

Uncle Roe's interest quickened. "What, all the way up on Crying Rock? What for?"

No way was I going to tell him about animal communicators and pet psychics. It would go through the department like wildfire and I'd never live it down. So I avoided his eyes and shrugged again. "She's a dog person. I wanted to talk to her, you know, find out more about her."

"Did you?"

"Did I what?"

"Find out anything?"

"Well, she's a lawyer. Guess you knew that. She's got a handful of sheep and a few other head of live-stock, nothing to call a working farm . . . has a mean cat. Boy, she spent a fortune remodeling that house, I can tell you that. She's in a wheelchair part of the time, with rheumatoid arthritis. I can't imagine why somebody who's sick would want to live way up there all by herself. It'd take an ambulance half an hour to get up the driveway in good weather. She talked about turning the farm into an animal sanctuary."

"Animal sanctuary?" Roe frowned. "What's that?"

"Oh, you know. It's a place that takes in sick and abused animals, rehabilitates them, or just gives them a place to live out their lives."

"What kind of animals?"

Again I shrugged. "Domestic ones, mostly. You have to have a special license for wildlife, so not many people get into that. Why are you asking? What's Sonny Brightwell got to do with any of this?"

"About what time were you up there today?"

"I don't know. I drove up there after I left you . . . maybe two o'clock?"

He jotted that down. "And what time did you leave?"

"An hour or so later. Cisco got into some mud and . . ." I frowned at him. "Come on, Uncle Roe, what's this about? Somebody just threw a gasoline bomb at my house, remember? And I can just about promise you it was not Sonny Brightwell who did it."

"Probably not," he agreed, "since about forty minutes before your call came in, somebody did the same thing to her."

I stared at him. "What? Is some maniac out there on a spree or something?"

"Doesn't look like it. So far, he seems to have just picked on you two."

I looked at Maude and then at Roe. "But—I don't understand. Why us?"

"Good question. Who've you girls pissed off lately?"

"Are you kidding me? I told you, I hardly even know the woman! She's a client, that's all, and hardly even a client—"

I broke off to shield my eyes as headlights blinded me, tires sprayed gravel and a car door slammed—all almost simultaneously. Buck came up the walk with a look on his face that reminded me why every woman he had ever assisted in or out of the line of duty promptly fell in love with him. He was dressed in civilian clothes—jeans, a sweater and a sheepskin-lined coat—and I remembered this was his day off. Remy Blonk, the dispatcher on duty when Maude dialed 911, must have called him at home, or someone from the office had.

Buck swept his eyes from Maude to me to the two dogs at my side and didn't waste his time with foolish questions.

"Are the rest of the dogs okay?" he said.

"They're fine," Maude said.

"I'm going to go check on them." I grasped the porch rail to struggle to my feet.

"I said they're fine." But Maude's grip on my arm was less to restrain than to assist me. I had to see for myself. She knew that.

I said, "Put Majesty and Cisco in the house, will you?"

Roe said, "You think about it. Let me know if you come up with anything."

"How about you letting me know if *you* come up

with anything," I returned. "This is crazy, just crazy."

Buck turned to Roe. "What the hell happened here?"

I hobbled off toward the kennel, trying to avoid uniforms and fast-freezing puddles, and by the time I got there my fear and confusion had turned to anger, and if I had had two good legs I think I would have kicked something—and probably broken my foot. My peace had been invaded, my home and my dogs threatened, and I had done nothing, *nothing* to deserve it. And what in the world did Sonny Brightwell have to do with it, if anything at all?

Or maybe—and this was what I really didn't want to think about—maybe her only involvement was by association with me. Maybe whoever had a grudge against me had been following me around and had decided to pick on Sonny simply to intimidate me. The woman was in a wheelchair, for God's sake.

I spent a few moments in the warm, fluorescent-lit office, taking deep breaths and trying to calm down before I went back into the kennel area. The heavy door muffled the sound of barking, but there were eight dogs back there and none of them were happy. The last thing they needed was my emotions to complicate their own.

When I was ready, I went from kennel to kennel, asking the dogs to sit and handing out dog biscuits,

keeping up a steady stream of soothing patter as I went. "I know, guy; you tell 'em, pretty girl. What did we ever do to anybody, anyway? How dare they come in here and wake you up with all their sirens and noises? I know; not your fault; it's all over now; just calm down; we've got it under control. Take it easy, pretty thing; you're a good girl, aren't you?"

Anyone overhearing might have thought I sounded a lot like Sonny Brightwell right then. But show me a trainer who doesn't talk to her dogs, and I'll show you a dog who doesn't know how to listen.

I came to the kennel of the border collie, who was backed into a corner in a crouch, barking a continuous, high-pitched, glazed-eyed bark. She was in a zone where nothing could reach her, dog biscuits meant nothing to her, and she couldn't even hear my voice. I couldn't leave her like that. For one thing, she was upsetting the other dogs, and we would be up all night trying to get them back to sleep if this kept up.

I unlatched the kennel and eased myself in. I left the crutch outside because I didn't want to scare her, although a smarter person might have brought it in as a defensive weapon. When she saw me she lowered her crouch even farther and her bark turned into a warning, snapping one.

I stopped all forward motion, and I said softly, "Easy, sweetheart. Nobody's going to hurt you here." Under normal circumstances, I would have crouched

down to make myself appear less intimidating, but with my leg in a brace that was not much of an option. Instead, I turned in profile to her and lowered my eyes. What I was saying, in dog language, was *I don't want any trouble here. I'm not going to fight you.* Whether she believed me or not was up to her.

"Calm down, girl, just calm down," I murmured. I tossed a dog biscuit toward the opposite corner of the kennel, trying to break her concentration, but she didn't even notice.

I stood my ground, talking softly to her, and the wild, threatening barking gradually changed to habitual barking, and finally to no barking at all. I drew a piece of cheese from my pocket and stood holding it in my open palm, watching out of the corner of my eye as the little dog crept closer and closer, and finally was nibbling out of my hand.

"There, now; you're not such a hard case as you like to pretend, are you? Do you think you can calm down and listen to reason now? No one is going to hurt you. Everything is going to be all right. That's a sweet dog."

I stood letting her lick my fingers, wondering whether this little dog, the only thing Sonny Brightwell and I had in common, really, could possibly be the key to this night's violence. I reached out my other hand to stroke her head, and suddenly the kennel door burst open behind me in a swirl of golden fur and happy panting breath.

I yelled, "Cisco, no!" and braced myself for a dog fight as Cisco bounded up to the border collie.

Cisco doesn't have an aggressive bone in his body, but I could hardly expect a potentially psychotic border collie whose kennel had just been invaded by a dog half again her size to know that. I was astonished, therefore, when the border collie did *not* lunge to defend her territory but instead accepted Cisco's invitation to play. They stood in a tail-waving standoff for a moment, and then, in a spinning, leaping, circling dance as energetic as that of any flamenco I had ever seen, began to romp the circumference of the kennel. On the second pass, they knocked me off my feet.

With no way to catch my balance, I would have fallen backward on the concrete and probably split my skull had not Buck caught me by the shoulders. Instead of thanking him I exclaimed, "Damn it, Buck, what did you bring Cisco out here for? He's supposed to be in the house!"

"What did you leave the kennel door open for?" he returned and handed me my crutch.

"Cisco, get over here!"

Cisco glanced at me, then executed a play bow to the border collie, and the two of them began another circuit around the kennel. As he passed me this time I caught his collar, swept him and Buck out of the kennel, put myself between the door and the border collie, and barely squeezed through be-

fore she did. I slammed the kennel door shut and latched it, and she barked at me indignantly. I glared at Buck.

"Guess what?" he said.

"Cisco, heel!" Cisco, who had started down the corridor to excite some more dogs, bounded back to me at once. I wish I could say it was the sound of my voice, but it was in fact the piece of cheese I pulled from my pocket.

"We got your man."

I stopped and stared at him. "What?"

"Your tax dollars at work. A patrol spotted Skete Jackson's truck in a ditch about half a mile down the road. He was drunk as a skunk, had half a can of gasoline, some empty Coke bottles and some fusing in the front seat. Let's talk about stupid, shall we? Not only couldn't he make a clean getaway, he could've damn well blown himself up in the process."

Skete Jackson was a neighbor of mine. His twenty acres adjoined my property on the south side, and in the middle of it he had set a single-wide with a satellite dish. He spent his time playing pool and his disability check on booze, and even though he might not be the most upstanding citizen in the county, he and I had never had a problem. The sense of hurt and betrayal I felt was so complete that for a moment I could only stare at Buck.

"Skete Jackson?" I repeated in a moment, when I could speak. "What did I ever do to him?"

Buck shrugged. "Maybe the barking dogs are keeping him awake."

"My dogs do not bark at night!"

"Maybe he's got something against single women in big white houses. Maybe your daddy sent him to jail for moonshining sometime back, or maybe . . ." We had been making our way at a slow, crutch-inhibited pace down the corridor toward the office, but the look he gave me now made me stop. "He heard about your adventures this afternoon, and what you found. It wouldn't be hard. It was all over the radio."

I struggled to get my mind around this idea. "You mean——because I found the gun?"

"To you, it might be a gun. To the rest of us, it's a murder weapon. And evidence."

It was all too much. My head was starting to throb in counterpoint to my knee. "But why would Skete Jackson care about . . ." And slowly his point began to dawn on me. As the person who had found the presumed murder weapon, I was now actively involved in the investigation. Topping the list of people who might wish me ill—or who would want to warn me to back off—would be the murderer. "Oh, come on, Buck, you can't think Skete would be involved in Luke Pickens' murder!"

"Why not?" We started walking again. Cisco, who had already forgotten his heel, was waiting for us at the office door. He knew that was where the

treats were kept, and his tail was wagging madly. "At this point, any suspect is more than we used to have."

"But—but what about Sonny Brightwell? Why would he pick on her? She doesn't have anything to do with finding evidence." And I thought guiltily, *Well, not really. At least, not much . . .*

Something of my uncertainty must have been evident in my voice, because Buck gave me an odd look. "Yeah, what about her? I mean, you called me up this morning wanting to know all about her, and next thing I know both of you are being targeted by some drunk with a match. What's with that?"

I released an exasperated breath. "Nothing. That's what I'm telling you."

"I thought you said you didn't even know her. That all she did was bring a dog in."

"I did. She did."

"Then what were you doing up there this afternoon?"

"Look, I already answered these questions to Uncle Roe. If you want real answers, why don't you ask Skete Jackson? And let me know what he says, will you?"

"Oh, we're asking all right." He opened the door for me. Cisco scooted inside, went straight for the desk and did a perfect sit with his gaze fixed on the treat drawer. "Right now, all they're holding him on is DUI. We'll get somebody in from the DA's office

tomorrow to question him. And you'll want to press charges, of course."

I muttered, "Yeah, I guess." But there was an awful lot about this that just didn't make sense to me.

Buck tossed his arm around my shoulder and gave me a quick squeeze. "What a day, huh? Come on, I'll help you lock up."

I slid away from him, trying to make the movement seem natural as I turned to lock the door. "So. Where've you been?"

"What do you mean?"

"Look at you." I gestured. "All dressed up, smelling like twenty-dollar cologne. . . . Maude tried to call you earlier."

"Oh, yeah?" He evaded the question. "What did she want?"

I double-checked the lock to the kennel area and hobbled toward the window, waiting for Buck to answer my original question. He reached the window before I did, checked the lock and said, "I went by to see Cindy Winston."

I looked at him in mild surprise. "On your day off?"

"She's an old friend." He was trying not to sound defensive and not doing a very good job. "She's just been through a terrible tragedy and there's nothing wrong with me stopping by to see how she is."

"Which tragedy do you think was most terrible?"

I spoke before I could stop myself. "Losing her boyfriend or losing her child?"

"Oh, come on, Raine, that's not even worthy of you." He gave the second window lock an angry jerk.

"All I mean is that Uncle Roe tried to call her this afternoon and she wasn't home."

"She's staying with her mother."

"I know that. And her mother didn't know where Cindy was. So it was her mother who ended up coming down to the station to identify the doll we found."

Someone had apparently filled him in on the details of the afternoon, because he showed no surprise at the information. "Just because she wasn't sitting by the phone—"

"What kind of mother *doesn't* sit by the phone when her child is missing, for heaven's sake?"

He turned eyes on me that were cool and distant, and the muscle that twitched in his cheek telegraphed his annoyance. "Do you really want to have this fight now?"

Cisco had turned his attention from the treat drawer to the two of us, looking anxiously from one to the other like a child caught in the middle of a disagreement between his parents. Suddenly I was very tired.

"No," I said. "I don't want to fight at all. Cisco, let's go." I started toward the door, leaning heavily

on the crutch. "If you and Cindy want to take up where you left off, it's none of my business. Really."

"Well, you're right about that much. But for your information, where Cindy and I left off was twenty years ago in high school, and I don't have any intention of taking up with anybody. Just in case you're interested. Now, what was Maude calling me about?"

"She wanted to know if you'd heard anything about the gun I found. But I guess if you haven't been around . . ."

"It was registered to Luke Pickens," he returned shortly.

I paused with my hand on the door handle. "Wow. Murdered with his own gun." The same gun he had used to shoot his girlfriend and force her and her child into the truck. The same gun that had presumably been in the truck with him as they all drove off. The same gun Cindy could have so easily grabbed if he had laid it on the seat for an instant while he, perhaps, negotiated a hard turn, or reached across to lock a door or even to unlock the door just before he pushed her out—if, in fact, anything like that had actually occurred.

But if she had killed Luke, why didn't she just say so? It would have been self-defense, after all. And if she had killed Luke, where was Angel?

Furthermore, if she was a suspect in the murder of Luke Pickens, she probably wouldn't be hanging

out with my husband, a police officer, on his day off.

Probably.

I said, with a surge of largesse that all but the most dim-witted would have found suspect, "Maybe I should go see Cindy myself. Offer my sympathies, see if there's anything I can do."

Buck was anything but dim-witted. He replied, watching me cautiously, "I'm sure she'd appreciate that."

"After all, I've been pretty much breaking my butt, not to mention my knee, to find her little girl. She'd probably like to thank me."

Again, his voice was restrained and his eyes were watchful. "Probably."

"She might even be able to tell me something that could help in the search."

"Police investigation is not your job, Raine." Now his voice was stern. "A normal person might take having a bottle bomb thrown in her yard as a hint. Maybe you'd better just stay home and rest your knee."

I said, "Get the door on the way out, will you, Buck? Cisco, heel."

To my very great surprise, Cisco fell into heel position beside me. I hit the light switch as I passed, leaving Buck in the dark.

Chapter Ten

"Hey." No one in the country ever identified themselves on the telephone, and it took me a moment to recognize the voice as that of Wyn, Buck's partner. "That no-account husband of yours wouldn't happen to be there, would he?"

"No." I glanced at the clock. It was a quarter to seven in the morning, and Buck's shift didn't start for another half hour. He was notorious for allowing himself exactly the amount of time it took for him to reach his destination on time, and not a second more. I, on the other hand, had been up since five thirty, feeding dogs and cleaning the kennels. "Did you try him at home?"

"Nah, it's not important. He was supposed to meet me for breakfast before our shift starts. I guess he forgot."

"Sounds like Buck. Are y'all on days now?"

"Just pulling in some overtime until some of this mess gets cleared up. I guess you heard they pulled us off the search."

"Yes." My voice was heavy. "It's been too long."

"We're still rotating teams out, but . . ."

"It's mostly recovery," I finished for her. Recovery, as opposed to rescue, was the stage of the search that turned from looking for a living victim to recovering the remains for burial.

"Meanwhile, we've still got a murder investigation going on, and the usual police business, so there's overtime. And that's what I called about."

"Overtime?"

"Police business. Are you coming down to the office later? We need you to sign a complaint."

"Yeah, I guess." Absently I pulled back the curtain, gazing down at Buck's driveway across the valley. Any minute now his dark blue pickup should round the corner on his way to work. "I don't know what time."

"Well, your perp confessed to throwing the bottle bomb, so there should be no problem holding him."

At that moment a car did round the corner of Buck's drive, but to my surprise it wasn't his. It was too far away to determine the make, but the bright citron yellow color was impossible to miss. Who was making cars that color, anyway? And who around here would own one?

I watched the little yellow car progress down the

half-mile gravel drive, bouncing over ruts and flinging up mud. Whoever it was, wasn't very particular
about the fancy paint job. "I don't suppose Skete
said why he did it, did he?"

"Not exactly. But he was mad as spit about some
land deal or another. Says you and that lesbian
lawyer are in cahoots to ruin him. I guess he's talking about Ms. Brightwell. Is she a lesbian?"

"I don't think so. How would I know? Magic, get
down!"

Magic had taken advantage of my momentary distraction to jump—literally—on top of the kitchen
table and help herself to the scraps of toast I had left
on my plate from breakfast. Cisco barked indignantly
and charged the table, with less intention of righting
a wrong than of scoring some toast for himself, I'm
sure, and about five seconds of minor chaos followed.
Magic snatched a last piece of toast, toenails screech-
ing on the tabletop, dishes clattering, and leapt off the
table, over Cisco's head. She raced past me and into
the living room with Cisco in hot pursuit.

A lot of people don't realize what incredibly tal-
ented jumpers Aussies are. That's only one of the
reasons that, when you have them, you can't take
your eyes off them for a minute.

I said, "I've gotta go, Wyn. So is that why Skete
Jackson tried to burn my house down? Because he
thinks Sonny Brightwell and I are lesbians?"

"You'd have to ask him. All I know is he's com-

pletely unrepentant, which is going to make some judge's job a lot easier."

"Okay, I'll be down before lunch. Oh, and Buck's on his way," I added as I saw Buck's pickup round the same corner the little yellow car had passed a moment ago. "Give him hell for standing you up."

"Bye, Raine."

I stood watching Buck's truck, frowning a little, as I hung up, and then a crash from the living room reminded me that I had more important things to worry about than what Buck was up to.

I knew I should have called Sonny last night— after all, Skete Jackson was *my* neighbor, and I somehow felt responsible for his unprovoked attack on her, even if it turned out to have nothing to do with me whatsoever. I had told myself that the hour was late, she was probably in bed, and there was nothing I could tell her, anyway. But this morning I really had no excuse. So I waited until eight thirty, which my mother had taught me was the earliest hour at which any well-mannered person made a telephone call to another, and I dialed the number that was written on her card.

She answered just as I was about to hang up, sounding a little out of breath. I identified myself and added, "I hope I'm not disturbing you."

"Not at all. I was outside. I had a little excitement here last night, and I was just trying to clean up."

I felt an immediate stab of guilt that I hadn't asked anyone last night what kind of damage Sonny had sustained. After all, she had animals too.

I said, "I know, and I'm terribly sorry. The same person who was at your place threw a bottle bomb over here too." She made a sound of horror and I added quickly, "No one was hurt here. Was there much damage at your place?"

"Fortunately, he hit one of the outbuildings I was planning to restore. Saved me the trouble of tearing it down."

"Well, they caught the guy. One of the locals, drunk and joyriding. He seems to think you're a lesbian."

"Well, I'm not but I guess that doesn't make much difference. Is that why he targeted your place too?"

"He seemed to think you and I were plotting against him somehow. I just talked to a sheriff's deputy and she said he was ranting about some land deal. The only thing is, I'm not involved in any land deals. Are you?"

Sonny was silent for so long that I thought we might have been disconnected.

I said, "Sonny?"

She said, "I think you'd better come to that meeting tonight."

"What meeting?"

"The one at the community center. It starts at

seven o'clock. I don't know how this all ties together, but I have a feeling it might not be over yet. "

Elsie Dickerson brought her Great Pyrenees, Gentle Ben, in for grooming every Friday at nine o'clock. Grooming is not something we specialize in here at the Dog Daze Boarding and Training facility, although Maude is better at it than I am, and our services are limited to bathing, combing out, and clipping nails. For most people around here, that's more than enough, especially in the winter when a 150-pound dog who hasn't had a bath in six months begins to put his house privileges at serious risk.

Elsie was conscientious about Ben's grooming, and I admired her for that. On the other hand, she didn't have much choice—he outweighed her by thirty pounds minimum, was snow-white and thick-coated and enjoyed digging mammoth mud pits in his spare time. To say he was high maintenance would be an understatement.

But there was a reason she called him Gentle Ben. The big dog came plodding into the office off leash, gave Maude and me a cursory glance in turn and promptly lost interest. He selected a rawhide chew from the bin by the door, took it to the corner and plopped down with a big sigh to chew.

In contrast, his caretaker came bustling in like a collection of loose parts blown together by the wind—hat askew, coat misbuttoned, carrying two

tote bags with items spilling out of both, missing one glove and trailing Ben's leash behind her. "I declare, I don't know some mornings how I get myself out the door. Do you know I lost my keys three times before I got to the carport? And then I couldn't find Ben's leash, not that he needs it, what a sweet boy, and I promised to take a load of books by the library and I never *did* find those, but I did find Ben's Kong toy. He likes to chew on it when he gets bored if you stuff it with cheese. Oh, dear, I didn't bring the cheese. I hope we're not late."

Maude and I looked at each other and grinned. "No, ma'am, you're not late," I said. "And we have cheese."

Maude relieved Elsie of Ben's leash and went to snap it on the big dog's collar. Fortunately, he wasn't the least bit protective of his treat and let her do as she liked. "Just the usual today, Mr. Ben? Shampoo and blow-dry? What a good dog."

"Oh, he's just been an awful boy this week. Look at him; he's filthy."

"We'll have him white as snow in no time, won't we, big guy?" Ben responded to Maude's gentle tug on his lead and got to his feet, bringing his rawhide chew with him.

I pushed myself out of my chair and got to my feet with much less grace than Ben had, using the furniture for balance as I stumped over to the desk

to check the schedule. "It's a pretty light day today. Do you want to pick him up about one?"

"That will give me just enough time to finish all my errands. Maybe I should run back by the house and try to find those books. . . . Now, where is your crutch, missy? I'm quite sure your discharge orders included using crutches whenever you are on your feet for at least the next ten days."

For all her scatterbrained appearance, Elsie was an excellent nurse. I looked at her sheepishly. "I guess I left them at the house."

She regarded me severely. "Well, you're just prolonging your recovery; you know that. You know who you should get to take a look at it? Dr. Jacob Stern. Best orthopedic surgeon in western North Carolina, and we were lucky to get him. You want a good doctor, you ask a nurse, and I'm telling you, he's the best."

"I'll remember that."

"Say good-bye to mum, Ben." Maude opened the door to the grooming room.

"Bye, sweetheart! Oh, wait, here's your Kong!"

She dug in one of her bags for the toy and I said quickly, as she started to run after Maude, "We'll keep it up here until we put him in the drying cage."

"Oh, good." She surrendered the toy. "Don't forget the cheese. I just think it's a crying shame about that poor child, and you practically ending up im-

mobilized trying to find her. I don't suppose they've heard anything?"

I shook my head. "They're still looking." I didn't feel it necessary to explain further, but Elsie was no fool.

"Well, they'll never find her. Not alive, anyway. It's just a crying shame. People like that shouldn't be allowed to have children, you ask me. I mean, she couldn't even decide who the father was when that child was born!"

I raised my eyebrows in surprise. I had never really given much thought to whom Angel's father might be; I suppose I had always assumed it was Luke Pickens. But Angel had been born six years ago and Cindy had dated a lot of different men before Luke Pickens . . . including, according to the local gossips, my husband.

Elsie gave a satisfied nod at my reaction. "It's a small hospital, you know, and there was such a fuss, you can't imagine. Cindy had the social worker back three times before she'd finally sign the birth certificate, and I heard she changed the name of the father every time."

"Who did she finally decide on?"

"You wouldn't believe me if I told you." Then she looked abashed. "Anyway, I probably shouldn't say. It's just what I heard; I didn't see it. I was working the surgical floor back then, and speaking of which, I'm going to get you Dr. Stern's card and you

call him, you hear? He can do laser surgery on that knee and have you running wind sprints in no time. One o'clock, you say? I'll see you then. Take care of my baby boy!"

And she breezed out the same way she breezed in, trailing objects behind her and leaving me, thoughtful and disturbed, in no mood to help Maude groom dogs.

I pulled up in front of the Winston house at nine forty-five. I refer, of course, to the home of Hazel Winston, widow of John Jay Winston, an upstanding member of the First Methodist Church, the Hansonville Garden Club, the Homemakers Club, and the Smoky Mountain Quilters. My mother used to say that a woman couldn't be held responsible for the lives her adult children chose. I remember hoping she wasn't referring to me.

The Winston home was a neat little saltbox on six acres, most of it craggy. The dirt drive made a U around a small square of snow-splattered brown lawn that was anchored by a big oak tree. A ten-year-old Ford that I figured belonged to Mrs. Winston was in the aluminum carport. In the center of the U, situated between potential visitors and the front steps, was a citron yellow two-door sedan. I parked behind it and took my time making my way to the front steps. At least I had my answer about who was making cars that color. Chevy. And this

particular car still bore the dealer's plates from Pickens Chevrolet-Pontiac-Dodge in greater metropolitan Hansonville.

Maude had wanted to come with me, and I could tell it irritated her to no end that Gentle Ben's bath was standing in her way. The truth was, now that I was here I regretted not having waited for her. And I wished I had brought a dog along. What had I been thinking? If there was anything more awkward than making a condolence call on your husband's ex-lover, I could not at that moment think what it was.

It was an old farmhouse, and the walls were not very thick. As I balanced on my crutch and prepared to knock on the glass-paned front door, I could hear angry voices coming from inside. I hesitated, groaning inwardly. Bad enough I had to try to think of something nice to say to Cindy Winston, but now I was obviously going to be walking into an unpleasant scene between her and her mother. Apparently they were so embroiled in their discussion that they had not heard me drive up. That's one good thing about having dogs: you're never surprised.

Then the voices became clearer as their owners apparently moved into the front room, and I paused with my hand inches from the doorframe, poised to knock. I listened without shame.

"It's—it's unseemly; that's what it is! Staying out all night, with your so-called boyfriend, if that's what he was, not two days in the grave—"

"Mama, I'm a grown woman! I can do what I please!"

"And your baby girl still lost out there somewhere! How can you even think about—"

"Mama, will you hush? You think I don't know it? Do you think I'm not worried? Angel's okay; I just know she is. Now, will you lay off me?"

"Lord help me, what kind of child did I raise? Where *were* you all night, Cindy? How can you go off whoring around—"

"I was *not*—"

I knocked firmly on the door.

Abruptly the voices ceased. In a moment the lace curtain at the windowed door parted, and in another moment the door swung open.

Hazel Winston wore a faded coral sweatshirt and baggy cotton trousers. Her gray pin curls looked squashed and flat, her plump face jowly, her complexion wan. Her eyes were red-rimmed and her lips thin and sunken with tension. She couldn't have been over fifty-six, but she looked eighty that morning.

I blathered, "Mrs. Winston, hi. I'm Raine Stockton—"

Her face relaxed almost immediately with recognition. "God bless you, child, I know who you are. Judge Stockton's daughter. You were out looking for our little Angel. Come in, dear, come in out of the cold." She reached for my hands with her hot, dry ones and pulled me inside.

I was immediately assaulted by a blast of hot air from the ceramic gas heaters, and a haze of cigarette smoke so thick it hung in the air like a storm cloud. Cindy Winston was hunched in a green tweed easy chair near the edge of the living room where it gave way to the open dining room, smoking gloomily. She barely glanced up when I came in.

She was wearing low-slung, painted-on jeans and a tight T-shirt that stopped just above the waistband of her jeans. Cindy had a figure that testified to a fast-food lifestyle: not fat, but certainly not that of a runway model either. I did not think the outfit was particularly flattering on her, but that's just me.

To be fair, she had a pretty face, big brown eyes and nice shoulder-length brown hair with way too much highlighting. Her left arm was in a green sling, and I could see a pale gauze bandage around her plump upper arm. She smoked in a rhythm that was counterpoint to the nervous tapping of her booted toe.

Hazel Winston fussed around, removing a neat pile of folded laundry from the sofa, offering to take my coat and trying to help with the crutch while I removed it, offering me coffee and in general making me realize that my condolence call, if that was what it was, was causing far more trouble than comfort. I wished I had brought a casserole or something.

Finally I was settled, though I had to twist around on the sofa to see Cindy. I said, "Cindy, I just wanted

to stop by and tell you that we've all been thinking about you. I can't imagine how hard this must be for you. I remember Angel from one of the school programs I did with my dog. She was so sweet."

There; that was nicely done. My mother had spent countless hours—maybe even decades—trying to imbue me with the niceties of civilized conversation, in hopes, I suppose, that my future would take me closer to the White House than the farmhouse, with the result that I had, somewhere in my repertoire, exactly the right thing to say for every occasion. Express sympathy but don't presume intimacy. Remark on some personal connection with the victim. Be genuine. I had worked hard on my speech all the way over here. And Cindy just glared at me.

Three or four beats of silence passed, and then her mother plunged in, tripping over her words in an effort to fill the void. "We just appreciate so much you—the police—I mean everyone, what you're doing, trying to . . . Well, it takes a village, doesn't it? What I mean is, it's just so hard . . ."

Her voice broke and her soft, sagging face crumpled even further. She fumbled in her pocket for a tissue. "She was such a sweet child," she murmured, her lips quivering. "So sweet . . ."

"Stop talking like she's dead, Mama!" Cindy's first words since I arrived were sharp and impatient. "She's not dead! For God's sake, give it a rest, will you?"

Now it was my turn to stare. And I have to say, all my mother's good manners went right out the window, and whatever genuine empathy I might have dredged up for Cindy Winston went with them.

I said, trying to modulate my tone, "Actually, Cindy, there was another reason I came over. As you know, I've been involved in the search"—and though, as anyone with half-normal vision could plainly see, I was no longer actively involved, I breezed right past that fact—"and I was hoping you might be able to help me understand more of what happened that night. Maybe if I had more information I might be able to help narrow the grid . . ." Just how stupid *was* Cindy, anyway? But I plunged on, my expression earnest, my determination undaunted. "I mean, I don't think any of us has ever had a really clear picture of just what happened that night. Maybe if you could go over it one more time . . ."

She flicked her cigarette butt into an old-fashioned standing glass ashtray and dug a crumpled packet from her jeans pocket. She barely glanced at me as she lit up again. "I already told the police everything I know. I don't have to tell it to you too."

"Yes, I know, but what I don't understand is exactly what the sequence of events was." I was aware of Hazel Winston's nervous glaze flickering from me to her daughter, like an anxious mother bird flit-

ting from one branch to another. I ignored it. "I mean, I know it's hard to think about now, but you were shot at your trailer, right? And then Luke forced you and Angel into his truck?"

She just smoked.

"So where were you, about, when he pushed you out of the truck?"

"Oh, for God's sake, I already went through this with the police! How the hell should I know? I was bleeding, for God's sake; I was shot! He pushed me out of a moving truck! I rolled into a ditch. I must've passed out. When I woke up I wandered around in the cold and dark until I saw lights from the highway, and I followed them all the way here to Mama's house. It took me hours."

"Mmm, that must have been awful," I murmured. "Where was Angel?"

If looks could kill, hers certainly would have imploded one of my vital organs. "What do you *mean*, where was she?" Her voice was subzero. "She was in the freakin' *truck* with a freakin' *maniac*; that's where she was. What are you even doing here, anyway? Don't you people ever talk to each other?"

Mrs. Winston said nervously, "Are you sure I can't get you some coffee, dear? It won't take but a minute to put the pot on."

"No, thank you, ma'am." I refocused on Cindy. "What I meant was, when you were pushed out of the truck—where was Angel? The truck has a bench

seat. Was she in your lap? Was she wearing a seat belt? Was Luke holding her while he was driving? I'm just trying to get a picture, here."

Silence. Hazel Winston stared at her daughter. Cindy stared at both of us, her expression cold. Finally, she said, "You're not with the police. A lot of people think you are, but you're just a girl with a dog. I don't have to talk to you."

I said, as pleasantly as I could, "You're right. You don't. I'm sorry if I upset you. I was just trying to help."

I reached for my crutch, and Hazel Winston bustled into action, fetching my coat, trying to help me to my feet. "Oh, no, dear, you're not upsetting us at all. We appreciate everything you all are doing, we truly do . . ."

I smiled at her gently. "I really hope we know something soon, Mrs. Winston."

I shrugged into my coat. "I love your new car, by the way. I've never seen one that color."

For a moment Hazel looked confused, then she said, "Oh, you mean the yellow one. No, that's Cindy's. She just got it last week."

I turned to Cindy, madly trying to do the math. A fancy new car like that, on a waitress's salary? And how much of a coincidence was it that her now-deceased boyfriend had a daddy who owned the dealership? I knew she must have seen the skepti-

cism in my eyes, but before she could react to it I said, "Wow, it's great. A Chevy, huh?"

She lifted her chin defiantly and inhaled smoke. "Yeah. It's a new model."

"Nice. I guess Luke got his daddy to give you a good deal."

"Luke? That skinflint?" She choked out a humorless laugh. "He never gave a crap about what I drove, and he sure as hell wouldn't go to his daddy about it if he did." She scowled suddenly, as though afraid she'd said too much, and stared at the tip of her cigarette. "Don't know what business it is of yours, anyway."

"None," I said as pleasantly as I possibly could. "None at all."

And somehow I managed to keep smiling as I said good-bye to Mrs. Winston, added something vague and hopeful about the search and made my way to my own car.

I stopped smiling the minute I passed the distinctive yellow car in which Cindy, according to her mother, had been out all night. And which I had seen at seven o'clock that morning leaving my husband's house.

Chapter Eleven

It wasn't that I cared one way or the other where Cindy Winston had been last night. Certainly it was none of my business with whom Buck chose to spend his time. But what I did care about—what made me, in fact, furious—was that he had lied about it.

Or maybe the thing that really upset me was the fact that I was surprised.

In that mood I might have been wiser to postpone my visit to the sheriff's office until later in the day. So naturally I drove straight there.

Only one news van was parked in Courthouse Square, and the amount of activity in and around the white-columned courthouse building was only a little more than normal for a cold gray March day—which is to say, almost none. I parked on the west side of the square, where the relatively new

Public Safety Building adjoined the eight-cell jail on one side and the courthouse on the other. Tourist money had paid for that building, and it was still a matter of hot debate, since most people thought the sheriff's department had been doing just fine in the basement of the courthouse for more than sixty years and didn't understand why the money couldn't have been put to better use.

I took the front entrance, which was handicap-accessible. I greeted Missy, who served as receptionist and paperwork organizer for the entire department, as I shrugged off my coat.

"Hey, Raine. How's the knee?"

"Coming along. How's it been around here?"

"Quieter, thank God. Most of the newspeople went home yesterday."

"Well, the media always has had a short attention span."

"Did you see the interview with Cindy yesterday noon?"

My interest sharpened. "No. I wondered why she hadn't been on, though."

Missy leaned forward confidentially. "Well, she didn't come off very well, if you ask me. Too much lipstick, not enough tears. She's a strange girl."

I was about to agree, and the telephone rang. Missy waved me toward the bullpen, which lay behind a set of closed wooden doors. "The sheriff is out, but Buck is back there. Go on in."

"Thanks, Missy."

Buck was on the phone when I came in, but he waved when he saw me. I turned away from him and spoke to Wyn, who was at the filing cabinet.

"Hey," she said. "It's been a crazy morning." She returned to her desk with a file folder. "Every time I get started on your complaint form, I get interrupted. Can you give me five minutes?"

"Sure." Buck was still on the phone. "Actually, I was wondering if I could talk to Skete while I was here. I mean, he is a neighbor of mine and this whole thing is just so weird."

She glanced at the clock, looking worried. "Well, it is still within visiting hours. But you're not going to change your mind about the complaint, are you? That Brightwell woman still hasn't shown up, and unless we get your signature we're not going to be able to hold him much longer."

"I thought you were holding him on suspicion of Luke Pickens' murder."

"He claims he has an alibi. If it checks out, we're going to have to drop that charge."

"It checks out," Buck said, hanging up the phone and rising from behind his desk. "At least a dozen people place him at the Palomino Bar and Grille over in Broward from eight to midnight, at which time he got into a fight, tried to crack a cue stick over some good old boy's head, and spent the rest

of the night in the Kane County jail. I'd say Skete is not having a very good week."

"Damn," said Wyn.

"Yeah," agreed Buck.

"I'd still like to see him." I avoided looking at Buck. "Can you call over to the jail and tell them I'm on my way? I'll stop back by to sign the complaint."

"Sure."

"Hey, wait up; I'll walk with you," Buck said.

"I know the way."

Buck looked as though he was going to ignore my response, as he so often did, but the phone on his desk started ringing again. With an annoyed expression he turned to answer it and I took advantage of the moment to slip past him and out the back door.

One thing about jails: No matter how nice they start out, or how much money the county puts into them, it doesn't take more than a couple of months before they all start looking the same. Our jail was only four years old, but already it looked like it had been here twenty years. The concrete floors were stained and scuffed, the institutional green walls chipped and faded, the porcelain sinks and toilets rusty looking. The whole place smelled like disinfectant and sweat and the usual other unpleasant substances. It was not a place in which I wanted to spend any more time than necessary.

The jailor led me to Skete's cell and asked me if I wanted him to wait. I didn't.

Skete, a thin man with a scruffy beard and bloodshot eyes, was lying on his cot. He swung his feet to the floor when I came up, and looked at me sullenly through the bars. "You gonna press charges?" he asked.

"You're damn right," I said.

He said something about high-and-mighty bitches who thought they owned people and I cut him off, my voice low and furious.

"You listen to me, you stupid son of a bitch. You could have killed somebody last night. And if you ever, I mean *ever*, try to hurt my dogs again, I'll come after you with a butcher knife and it won't be your ears I'll be looking to cut off, do you understand me?"

He glared at me, but there was an uneasiness in his tone that let me know he had gotten my point. "I ain't never tried to hurt a one of your dogs. I ain't no dog killer."

To some people that might have seemed an odd paradox—that a man who had admitted throwing a bottle bomb with the apparent intent to do harm to a person and/or her property would take pride in the fact that he would never harm a dog. But to me it made perfect sense.

I challenged, "Then what in God's name *were* you trying to do, Skete? I've never done anything to

you! You remember that time your coon dog got loose and got hit by a car in front of my house? He would've died if I hadn't wrapped him up and taken him to the vet!"

"Well, yeah," he admitted reasonably. "That was right neighborly of you."

"I've *always* been a good neighbor to you! And this is how you return the favor? By trying to blow up my house?"

"I ain't tryin' to blow up nobody's house! But maybe you oughta think twice before you go tryin' to cheat a man outta what he's got comin'. Just because your daddy used to be a big shot don't mean you got the right—"

"What in the world are you talking about?"

"You and that fancy lawyer lady, you think you hold all the cards. Well, I'm here to tell you there's some folks in this county that ain't gonna put up with it, and I'm one of 'em! Maybe I only got a couple of acres, but they're mine, you hear, to do with what I want! Damn bleedin' hearts and tree huggers, coming up here tellin' us what we can and can't do with our own damn land—"

I said, "Nobody's trying to tell you what to do with your land. And nobody's going to cheat you out of anything."

"You're damn right they ain't!"

For a moment we seemed to be at an impasse; he glared at me and I glared at him and neither one of

us seemed to know where to go next. Then I said, "Just tell me one thing. Who told you that Sonny Brightwell and I were trying to stop you from doing whatever it is you want to do with your land?"

He snorted and spit on the floor. "Reese Pickens, that's who. And he oughta know."

"Reese?" I couldn't hide my surprise. "What has he got to do with anything? What are you talking about?"

But Skete just stared at me. "You know just what I'm talkin' about, little lady. And I'll tell you somethin' else—I'm done talkin' about it. Get on outta here."

And with that he flopped down on his back on his cot, folded his arms across his chest and closed his eyes.

The interview, for what it was worth, was apparently over.

I limped back through the covered walkway to the sheriff's office and was relieved to see that Buck was not at his desk. I lost no time in signing the complaint form Wyn pushed at me. "The man's got a screw loose," I told her. "Jail's the safest place for him. And by the way, if he starts whining about me threatening him with bodily harm if he ever comes near my dogs again, he's lying."

She grinned at me as she tucked the form into a folder. "I never heard a word."

It was only a couple of hundred feet from the Public Safety Building to the courthouse records room, and it would have taken me longer to limp to my car, haul myself in, drive next door and re-park than it would to walk—even though walking was not exactly an easy accomplishment either. I hadn't taken more than a couple of dozen lurching steps down the walkway that separated the two buildings when I spotted Buck. Some days you just can't win for losing.

In typical macho fashion, he hadn't put on a coat, and he shoved his hands into his uniform pockets and hunched his shoulders against the wind as he came toward me. "I had to run some papers over," he said, nodding toward the courthouse. "You all done?"

"Yeah."

"I'll walk you to your car."

"I'm not going to the car."

I tried to move around him, and he blocked me. "What's the matter with you?"

What the hell. My day couldn't get any worse.

So I looked him in the eye and I said, "I went to see Cindy this morning."

Warily, "That was nice of you."

"Anything you want to tell me, champ?"

He frowned, hunching his shoulders even further against another gust of wind. "Like what?"

"All right. Let's try it this way. Did anyone ever

Donna Ball

think to ask Cindy where Angel was when Luke pushed her—Cindy—out of the car? Think about it, Buck. It's a bench seat. The kid had to be either sitting in her mother's lap or in the middle, between Luke and Cindy. If she was sitting near the door, she would have fallen out when the door was opened. So Luke had to either reach over Angel, unlatch the door and push Cindy out, or wrestle Angel from her mother's arms, unlatch the door and push Cindy out—all from a moving vehicle. Didn't anyone think that might have been a little hard to do? Didn't anyone question her story?"

"I told you, I didn't interview her. I—"

"Well, maybe there's a good reason for that."

He swiveled sharply to avoid another sharp blast of wind, shivering. "Jesus, Rainey, it's freezing out here. If you've got something to say, could you say it inside?"

"I'm in a hurry."

I started forward, and he caught my arm. If I could have gotten my balance I think I would have swung my crutch at him.

He demanded, "Will you tell me what's eating you? What the hell did you mean by that last crack?"

I jerked my arm away. "What I meant was, Cindy was lying about what happened that night. Nobody pushed her out of a moving car while her little girl stayed inside. And if she lied about that, what else

170

did she lie about? What I meant was, I wonder what your boss would say if he knew about your relationship with a potential suspect in a murder case." Oh, God, sometimes I hate myself. But once the torrent of words started, they came flooding out like venom, and I couldn't stop them. "That maybe if he's looking for a motive in Luke's murder he ought to be thinking about the good old-fashioned love triangle. And maybe he should be asking what *you* were doing when Luke was killed!"

Buck's eyes, normally a mild gray, went black. The expression within them was somewhere between incredulity and fury. "I was *working*, for God's sake! As you, Roe and everybody else in this county knows. What the hell are you trying to imply?"

"I *saw* her, Buck!" I exploded, heedless of the why or wherefore. "Why can't you just for once in your life be honest about it? I saw her!"

His expression, if possible, grew even more baffled. "Saw who? What are you talking about?"

"Oh, for crying out loud!" I swung away from him, and then, because I just couldn't walk away as long as he had any possible doubt, however faint, about his own guilt, I swung back. "Cindy's mother said she was out all night 'whoring around.' Those are her words, not mine. At seven o'clock this morning I saw her car leaving *your* driveway. What kind

of idiot couldn't connect the dots to who she's been whoring around *with*?"

And that was it. Even I couldn't stand myself any longer. I swung away and stumped off toward the courthouse, leaving a stunned and incredulous Buck in my wake.

I stood in the vestibule of the courthouse for a good five minutes, breathing deeply, trying to get the heat out of my cheeks and the foul taste out of my mouth, hoping to high heaven I wouldn't run into anyone I knew. I felt stupid, small, embarrassed and ridiculous. My mother would have been ashamed of me. I was ashamed of me. I wanted to crawl in a hole somewhere and die—but not before I took a baseball bat and knocked a few holes in a wall somewhere. Buck had always had that effect on me. Looks like I would have found a way to get over it by now.

Every time the front doors opened, I expected Buck to come striding in to make things right. He never did.

Finally, I took a deep breath, squared my shoulders and removed my coat. Moving with an awkward attempt at ease I had never been further from feeling, I made my way to the records office.

I waited in line behind a man who was trying to clear up a title dispute and a woman who couldn't understand why she had to go all the way across

the hall to settle her property tax bill. When I arrived at the counter, I leaned on it and smiled wearily.

"Hey, Sue Ann," I said. She and I had gone to high school together. "Listen, if I wanted to look at a birth certificate, could you help me out?"

She shook her head. "You want a copy of your birth certificate, you have to write to Raleigh. I have a request form, though." She reached under the counter for the form, but I stopped her.

"No, I don't need a copy. I just want to check something. Don't ya'll keep copies somewhere of all the babies born in the county?"

"What year?"

I did a rapid calculation and hoped I was right. "Oh, 2000, 2001."

"Hold on."

She disappeared into a room behind the counter and returned at length with a big black ledger marked *1995–2005*. "You can't take it out of the office," she warned before handing it over. "There's a counter over there where you can look at it."

My knee was on fire, but I smiled wanly as I gave up my hopes of being able to sit and rest for a while. I dragged the big book over to the counter Sue Ann had indicated and started to flip pages.

The first thing I realized was that Hanover County was apparently undergoing a population explosion. Who would ever have thought there

could have been that many babies born in this small county in the past ten years? The second thing I realized was that the entries were chronological, not alphabetical. Page by page, day by day, I flipped through the year 1999, then 2000. Finally, in September, I found it.

Angel Winston, female, born September 21, 2000, Middle Mercy Hospital, Hanover County, North Carolina. Mother, Cynthia Marie Winston, age 27. Father . . .

I stared at the name typed there, not knowing whether to feel relief or astonishment, and in the end, not knowing what to make of it at all. This explained a lot. And it explained nothing.

I stood frowning over the page until I started to get a headache. Finally, I closed the heavy book and trudged back over to the desk with it.

"Thanks, Sue Ann," I said distractedly and started to turn toward the door. But there was no one in line, and it wouldn't hurt to have a look.

"Say, Sue Ann," I said. "Could I have the plat book with Daddy's property in it?"

"Stockton Place Road? Wait a minute; I have to look up the lot number. . . ." She typed a few numbers into her computer, paged down some screens and disappeared again into the little room, returning with yet another oversized ledger, this one bound in blue.

"This is a popular book," she commented as she

handed it over. "You're about the fourth person to ask for it in the past two weeks."

I hesitated as I turned the book around. "Oh, yeah? Who else?"

"Well, first there was some big shot from Atlanta, all dressed up in one of those fancy suits like you see in the drugstore magazines. I don't know what he wanted. Then there was Skete Jackson, if you can believe that. I didn't even know he could read. And Frank Marrit."

"The lawyer?"

"Yeah. He was doing a title search. You getting ready to sell some lots, Raine?"

"No, not me."

"Too bad. You got some awful pretty pieces over there, especially 'longside the waterfall."

I wasn't about to haul the giant ledger over to the counter, so I opened it right there on the desk, paging forward until I found my property. I wasn't sure exactly what I was looking for in the blueprintlike survey maps. I found the road that was named after my family. I saw the big triangular-shaped plot bordered by streams and waterfalls and elevations, forty-six acres marked STOCKTON. At the back end of it, joined only by a hundred feet or so and a dotted line, was a little square labeled JACKSON. And across the road, adjoining my property at only one corner, separated by another one of those dotted lines, was a big, rambling plot labeled PICKENS.

It took me a lot longer to connect these dots than it had to make the connection between one yellow car and one unfaithful husband. There was a lot of flipping back and forth, reading legends, asking questions that Sue Ann was only too happy to answer. But finally it started to make sense.

And just when I thought my day couldn't get any worse.

Chapter Twelve

The night turned bitter, and there were only about twenty-five concerned citizens gathered in the big, drafty meeting room at the community center. Of course, I'm not too sure how many would have shown up for a meeting like this even if the weather had been pleasant. The truth is, I'm not sure how many people in the county—including me—even knew what it was about. By the time Maude and I arrived, fifteen minutes late, I was already wishing I had stayed home.

I felt bad about dragging Maude out in the cold, but she refused to let me drive alone, and she was probably right. I had spent so much time on my feet today that my knee was swollen past the point of even the smallest degree of flexibility, and I could barely get into the passenger seat of a car, much less drive it. But after I'd shared with Maude the infor-

mation I had gathered from my adventures of the morning, she had agreed that this was not a meeting we should miss.

I let the swinging door swoosh closed behind me and stood there for a moment, glancing around for familiar faces. There weren't many. The woman at the podium was Barbara Something-or-other ... well dressed, middle fifties, nice enough, but not local—which is to say, she and her husband had lived in the community only about ten years. I nodded to Bobby Rich, from the paper, who looked bored and ready to leave, and smiled at Dexter Franklin, who was on the county board of commissioners. He didn't look very happy to be there either. Other than a couple of real estate agents and Sonny, who sat near the front and flashed a welcoming smile at me when I entered, the only other person I recognized well enough to call by name was Reese Pickens.

His son was barely in the grave, and he was attending a community meeting? Maude and I shared a surprised look, and I guessed we weren't the only ones to be taken aback by his presence.

The big room was half filled with folding metal chairs, but most of them were empty. Everyone sat huddled up front in their coats, holding cups of coffee and trying to look interested in what Barbara was saying—everyone except Reese, that is. He sat two rows back from everyone else, on the aisle, next

to two men in expensive camel overcoats with brief-cases whom I immediately took for lawyers. He looked relaxed, well groomed and politely attentive to the speaker—not at all like a man whose last surviving son had just been murdered. Maude touched my arm and jerked her head toward the empty row of seats across the aisle from Reese. We weren't exactly quiet about seating ourselves, but Reese didn't even glance our way as we took the chairs across from him.

"And so, without further ado," Barbara was saying, "allow me to introduce to you Sonora J. Brightwell, attorney at law, who has so generously agreed to donate her time in support of our cause. Ms. Brightwell."

She lifted her hands in quick, light applause, and a polite spattering of others joined. Sonny, leaning heavily on a padded metal cane, made her way to the podium, while Barbara pulled down a projection screen and arranged it to the left of the speaker's stand.

Sonny looked professional but approachable in a gray tweed suit and a pale blue blouse with a soft, floppy bow at the throat. Her hair was twisted up and pinned softly to frame her face, and she wore pearl earrings. Maude glanced at me and nodded her approval. I had to agree—the woman knew her audience. She looked feminine enough to be non-

threatening but smart enough to be credible. Nicely done.

She glanced toward the back of the room and gave a little nod, and two of the three banks of fluorescents went out, leaving the room dark enough for projection. She pushed a button in her hand and a picture appeared on the screen of a picturesque ocean wharf, dotted with shrimp boats and fish markets. Her voice came through the darkness. "Let me tell you a story about a little seacoast town called Henry's Cove. The population wasn't much more than all of Hanover County. It had a grocery store, a couple of gas stations, a mom-and-pop restaurant where people gathered to catch up on all the gossip about their neighbors . . ." As she flashed the slides of comfortable-looking hometown streets, weathered but well-kept houses, people having meals at the Formica-tabled booths in the diner, I could sense the smiles going around the room. It all looked familiar and welcoming.

"Not so different from your community here. Most of the families made their living in the fishing industry, and you might not know that's one of the hardest jobs in the world." She showed a series of shots of oyster bars and rusty shrimping boats, men, women and children in stocking caps mending nets, coarse-skinned women in rubber aprons and gloves behind long wooden trestles piled with oyster shells.

In contrast, there next came a slide of a sparsely occupied sugar white beach in high summer, a boy tossing a stick for a black Lab while his parents lounged on chairs in the sand. In the background was a stretch of dunes, and beyond them a coral and turquoise beach house on stilts. It could have been propaganda from the chamber of commerce, right down to the Labrador retriever—which, as everyone knows, is the number one most popular breed in the United States today. She followed this with a shot of a neat-looking, sixties-style motel with a well-occupied parking lot, and of a three-story Victorian-style bed-and-breakfast with a koi pond in the front. Again, chamber of commerce stuff. "Of course, a few lucky people were starting to discover this little piece of paradise on earth, and tourism played a healthy, although not particularly significant, role in the economy."

It sounded a lot like Hansonville. I thought I knew where she was going with this, and I started to feel a little queasy.

"As the price of fuel got higher and the cost of importing fish from other countries got lower, more and more of these families started to struggle. Still, they mananged to keep themselves employed, send their children to school, support their churches.

"In 1998, the average income for a family of four was about twenty-eight thousand dollars. Not so great. But most owned their own homes, and prop-

erty taxes on most of those homes were less than two hundred dollars a year. The average resale value on a three-bedroom, two-bath house on an acre of land with a view of the bay was fifty-eight thousand dollars. Not too bad."

She showed a slide of a residential street featuring a neat brick home on a spacious lot with a nice lawn and a swing set in front. In the background was a sliver of blue, which was, presumably, the bay. What a bargain.

"In 2003, the average family income was nineteen thousand five hundred dollars. The number of full-time residents had decreased by half. The average cost of a three-bedroom, two-bath home was four hundred and eighty-five thousand dollars. . . ." A shocked murmur rippled through the crowd. "And property taxes for the average homeowner were over nine thousand dollars a year—that's almost half the annual income. People were forced to sell their homes to pay their taxes, only to discover they couldn't afford to buy another house in the community in which they had lived all their lives. Businesses that had been operating for generations closed their doors because they could no longer afford the rent on their own buildings." For emphasis, she flashed a slide of a run-down stucco building with a CLOSED sign in the window. Weeds were growing up through cracks in the sidewalk, and brambles had overtaken a nearby fence.

"The county budget allowed for a salary of fourteen thousand five hundred dollars per annum for a first-year schoolteacher. That same schoolteacher could not find housing for less than ninety-five hundred dollars per year. Guess what happened to the school."

We didn't have to guess. She showed us a slide of an abandoned schoolyard overgrown with weeds, broken swings hanging from chains, and in the background a building with broken windows and missing shingles. It was sobering to say the least. Incredible, to say the most.

"What happened, you wonder." The screen went dark. "What could have happened to turn this charming, unspoiled town with its abundance of natural resources and its dedicated, hardworking population into a ghost town in five short years?"

Suddenly there flashed on the screen a waterfront scene crowded with stark white monoliths. It took us all a moment to realize that what we were seeing was the same view she had shown us at the beginning of the presentation. Only instead of shrimp boats and fishing piers, docks and fish houses, the shore was wall-to-wall condos, stretching as far as the eye could see. A murmur, like a collective moan of grief, went through the crowd.

"Somebody figured out they weren't making any more waterfront property," Sonny said. The ugly slide of condominiums blotting out the sky re-

mained on the screen. "Somebody offered this fisherman a million and a half dollars for his wharf. He'd never made more than thirty thousand a year in his whole life. Do you think he was going to say 'No, thank you'? Of course, each one of these condominium buildings is now worth about twenty-two million, but who's counting? Only the people who are paying the taxes on houses that have been in their families for eighty, ninety years and which, five years ago, were appraised at one-tenth of what they are being valued at now. Only the people who once owned their own businesses but who are now lucky to get a minimum-wage job cleaning houses or mowing lawns for the influx of seasonal millionaires who have taken over their town. Only the people who remember mile-long beaches and porpoises offshore and clear water in the bay. That's all gone now. What they have instead are exhaust fumes and fast-food restaurants and a sewage treatment plant that, unfortunately, has been cited twice in the past five years for dumping into the bay. A good portion of those nine-thousand-dollar-a-year property taxes went toward paying the fines, but that's okay—there's more where that came from. Sadly, however, the fines did not bring the fish back, or the porpoises that fed on them, or the clear blue water that had surrounded this little peninsula for thousands of years. May I have the lights, please?"

We all sat there, blinking, in stunned silence as

the banks of fluorescents flickered back on, one by one. Sonny rested one arm on the lectern, her demeanor composed, her tone earnest. "Ladies and gentlemen, you are here because you care about this county; you care about your homes. You care enough to work together to keep what happened to Henry's Cove from happening here. And I'm here to tell you that all the ingredients for a similar disaster are already in place. You have a local population that is subsisting, for the most part, at or below the national poverty level. You have a vast wealth of natural resources held in the hands of a desperate, uneducated local population. You have a greedy developer who has just figured out that—guess what?—they are not making any more mountains. He is prepared to offer these locals more money in one day than they are likely to earn in a lifetime, and once the first acre is sold, there will be no closing the lid on Pandora's box. These people must be protected from themselves. We must encourage sustainable development from the outset, to show the locals that there is a way for progress and nature to live side by side. And that's what I'm here to help you do."

"Jesus," I muttered under my breath to Maude, "I'm starting to understand why Skete threw that firebomb."

Maude poked me sharply in the ribs and I shut up, but my stomach was churning. We had already

agreed that I had made enough of a target of myself by simply showing up here, and the least heard from me the better. But I have to be honest. If I hadn't put the safety of my dogs first and foremost, I would have been hard-pressed to stay silent that night.

Sonny went on for some time about causes of action, injunctions, developmental models. She had charts and graphs, and none of it made much sense to me, probably because I was an uneducated local who was living below the national poverty level. Finally, she concluded to a hearty round of applause, and Barbara came to the podium again, holding Sonny beside her with an arm around her shoulders.

"Thank you, Ms. Brightwell," she gushed. "I can't tell you how grateful we are to have a person of your caliber volunteer to help spearhead our campaign to save our beloved mountains." Said the woman who had only lived here for ten years, and who had paid off her picturesque, thirty-two-hundred-square-foot log cabin home, which included three stone-encased garden whirlpool tubs and granite countertops in the kitchen, in cash with proceeds from her dot-com stock and had plenty left to furnish the place with the best High Point had to offer—*and* hire a decorator. I frowned and wriggled in my seat. "Now, if anyone has any questions, I'm sure Ms. Brightwell will be happy to answer them."

"I have one."

To my surprise, the voice belonged to one of the men sitting beside Reese Pickens, across the aisle from me. He stood up, smiling pleasantly. "Allow me to introduce myself. My name is Charles Brockett, and I represent the greedy developer in question. I wonder if I might be allowed to present an accurate depiction of what it is, exactly, we propose to do? After all, this *is* a public meeting, isn't it? I think the public deserves to have the facts—all the facts."

A buzz went through the crowd and two dozen angry, suspicious faces turned to face the speaker as he made his way toward the podium with his briefcase. Reese Pickens folded his arms and looked smug. Barbara stammered and stuttered and said nothing. Sonny sat down with what I thought was a rather admirable display of grace under pressure. I glanced at Bobby, who had lost that bored look and was furiously scribbling notes for this week's edition of the paper, and I murmured to Maude, "Woohoo. Here we go."

Chapter Thirteen

For emotional appeal, Mr. Charles Brockett's presentation wasn't nearly as effective as Sonny's had been. But the wow factor was off the charts. With the efficiency of a battlefield general, he, with his assistant, set up folding easels and a laptop computer with a PowerPoint presentation. We saw charts and graphs, population grids, infrastructure maps, all of them very quickly. We heard promises like 8.2 million dollars in water and sewer improvements, 3 million for schools, two hundred new jobs—and then he brought out the pièce de résistance. Although I had guessed, from my research that afternoon, that something like this was coming, I must say that even I was struck dumb by the video that the computer generated onto the screen.

The production was worthy of Disney in its high-tech special effects. The movie that appeared on-

screen was of a familiar wooded mountain the spring—a wild, tumbling waterfall, clear streams bouncing over smooth rocks, deer grazing in a glade and in the background the picturesque white spire of First Methodist Church, and beyond it, layers upon layers of Blue Ridge Mountains. I knew that view well, since I had climbed that very mountain most every day of my childhood. In one shot, in fact, the camera panned over west and I could see the chimney that defined my own roofline. The video had been shot on Hawk Mountain, which adjoined my property.

In the plat book, it had been the plot marked PICKENS.

My brows drew together in incredulous concentration as the scene morphed subtly and, through the magic of computer-animated design, a brilliant velvet green golf course appeared, winding its way gently across the mountaintop. Deer still grazed in wooded glades, and somehow it appeared as though not a single tree had been cut. Streams still bounced and tumbled down rocky beds, and waterfalls splashed into crystal blue lakes. As our tour continued, classical music swelled, and we saw a magnificent glass and stone country club, Tudor-style mansions tucked discreetly into deeply wooded lots, an airport, a helipad. The more I looked, the more amazed—and relieved—I became. For a while I had thought this developer, whoever

he was, might be a real threat. But this was a pipe dream.

"As you see, our plan is very environmentally conscious. Your natural resources are our natural resources, and we are sparing no expense to protect the beauty of this area." He went on for a while about safeguarding the waterways from chemical runoff, preserving habitats. Sonny bombarded him with questions, and he had an answer for each one.

"The county board of commissioners and the Hansonville Chamber of Commerce have already seen our presentation and look upon our proposal with great favor," added Mr. Brockett. He smiled out into the audience. "I hope I'm not speaking out of turn, Commissioner Franklin."

So that's what he's doing here, I thought, straining in my seat to see Dexter Franklin. *He's acting as front man for the commissioners.*

"I think it could be the best thing that ever happened to this county," declared Franklin uncategorically. "It'll put us on the map."

Dexter Franklin owned a construction company, and the only earth-moving equipment in 150 miles. A construction project the size of this one could very well be the best thing that had ever happened to him.

Sonny said, "Mr. Brockett, are we to assume you've already purchased all the land you need for this project?"

"We have begun to make acquisitions, yes. But of course there are a lot of details to be ironed out yet."

"And might I ask how much you're offering per acre?"

He chuckled. "Do you have some property you want to sell, Ms. Brightwell? Purchase prices will become part of the public record after closing."

"How much property do you intend to acquire?"

"About three hundred acres."

"And what about roads? What kind of access do you plan for your resort?"

"Actually, we expect to have very little impact on the county road system, since this will be primarily a fly-in community."

Maude and I exchanged a look. A fly-in community? In Hansonville? Oh, yeah, *that* was going to happen.

Sonny kept asking him questions, and he kept answering them, and I could tell none of it was going quite the way the Save the Mountains group had hoped. The guy was coming off as a real environmental sweetheart, and Sonny's original point about the impact that rapid growth and inflated land values could have on a community was completely lost. Not that it mattered, of course. None of it was going to happen.

But that wasn't important as long as the people who had land to sell *thought* it was going to happen. People like Reese Pickens.

It was close to ten o'clock by the time the meeting broke up, and people still didn't seem ready to leave. Maude murmured to me, "If you're going to be okay here for a minute, I'm going to try to cozy myself up to the charming Mr. Brockett."

"Good plan. I think I'll have a few words with the not-so-charming Mr. Pickens."

Reese was standing with Dexter Franklin at the back of the room, both of them looking a little too smug for my liking. When he saw me approaching, Dexter slapped Reese on the back, said something about seeing him later and slipped out the door. Reese just stood there, hands in the pockets of his sheepskin-lined suede coat, and waited for me to reach him.

Like both his sons had been, Reese was a good-looking man, well over six feet tall with a full head of thick silver hair and a strong, weathered jawline. Supposedly, he was as much a ladies' man as Luke had been, and he didn't treat his conquests much better than Luke had, either.

I said, sticking out my hand, "I'm sorry for your loss, Reese. I meant to come by sooner."

He eyed me skeptically, but a man's instinct, when a woman offers her hand, is to take it. He pulled his hand out of his pocket to shake mine, and seemed to remember it was bandaged at the same moment I noticed the fact. He shrugged and stuck his hand back into his pocket.

"Doing some remodeling around the place," he said. "Caught my hand on a saw blade."

"That sounds serious."

"It's okay. No stitches."

I said, "Why did you tell Skete Jackson I was going to try to stop this land deal? I assume that's what he's all fired up about. Brockett must have tried to make him an offer."

He smiled, but there was no warmth in his eyes. "Yeah, I heard you had a little trouble down at your place. That Skete is one son of a gun, isn't he? A misunderstanding, that's all."

I nodded my head in a vague way toward the crowd that was still surrounding Brockett. "So all of this is your baby?"

"Not all." Pleasant smile, cold and wary eyes.

"But you're the one who's selling off pieces of Hawk Mountain."

"My land. Got a right to do with it what I want."

"I guess." Then I smiled. "You know this whole golf course, fly-in thing is never going to happen, don't you?"

A corner of his mouth turned up in a sly grin. "Not my problem. As long as the check don't bounce, I'm good."

"Glad to hear it. Because I'd hate to think what Brockett's people are going to have to say to you when they find out what you've done."

His expression remained unchanged. "Why, Miss

Rainey, I don't have the first notion what you're talking about."

I did not smile. "There's only one way to get construction equipment up that mountain, Reese, and that's on the Old Falls Road. The only problem is, that road runs across my property. And you don't have right-of-way. And I don't care how many firebombs you get Skete Jackson and his cronies to throw, you're not getting it."

He chuckled, shaking his head. "Raine Stockton, your daddy was one of the smartest men I ever knew. Too bad none of it got handed down to you. Skete Jackson got out of jail this afternoon, and the first thing he did was collect a nice, fat check for his little piece back behind you. Sugar pie, we don't need your right-of-way. We got Skete's land now, and we can build our own road."

I just stared at him, uncomprehending.

He chuckled. "The thing is, he wasn't inclined to sell at all until I told him how you were fixing to queer the deal for everybody. He got wind that there was a big developer involved and I guess he was thinking of holding us up for more money. Then I happened to mention as how the value of his land had already started to go down on account of how we were going to have to build a road to go around your place. Well, now, who could've guessed he'd do a damn fool thing like he did? But it all worked out all right, now, didn't it? We got the

shortest, quickest route up the mountain, you don't have to worry about having ole Skete for a neighbor anymore and Skete's off to buy himself a nice double-wide and a piece of creek property—if he can stay out of jail long enough to clear a lot. So what are you frowning about? Like I said, everything worked out just fine."

He tipped his hat to me as he went out the door, leaving me shivering in the blast of cold air and feeling every bit as stupid as he had accused me of being. Stupid, and utterly baffled. Here was a man whose only son had been murdered less than a week ago, and he had continued wheeling and dealing—and remodeling his house—without blinking an eye. He had conceived and executed that entire slippery plan to get Skete's little parcel of land, and all this had been going on right under my nose and I hadn't had a clue.

I made my way to the front of the room, where I saw Sonny calmly packing up her slides and her notes. She smiled when she saw me and I returned a sympathetic expression. "Guess you got blind-sided," I said, nodding toward the crowd that was still lingering around Brockett.

She laughed a little. "Not really. This is just the first volley. The real fight hasn't even begun. And he gave me more information in forty-five minutes than I've been able to get out of his company in six months."

I was surprised. "Six months? This has been in

the works that long and we didn't know anything about it?"

"Oh, sure. These things take years in the planning process, and the public announcements aren't usually made until a few months before they break ground."

"You sound pretty sure this thing is going to come off."

"Why shouldn't I be?"

"Well, for one thing," I said, laughing, "who's going to play golf on that million-dollar course up in the sky? Skete Jackson? Who's going to live in those high-priced mansions and fly their private jets into the airport?"

"John Travolta," she replied calmly. "He has a private jet and plenty of money to fly it wherever he wants to. Senators and congressmen, sultans and princes and presidents of foreign countries, Coca-Cola and IBM and Microsoft. These aren't private homes they're building; they're corporate assets. And by the way, that golf course is going to cost a lot more than a million dollars."

I frowned. This was starting to sound a little less like a pipe dream and more like a real, although barely imaginable, possibility. "But these things take time, right? I mean decades. And a lot can go wrong before the first shovelful of dirt is turned."

She smiled sympathetically. "Sometimes," she agreed. "And that's what I'm here for—to make sure things go as slowly as possible."

I spent a few unsettling moments pondering the implications of all I had learned tonight, and then I forced my thoughts back to the present.

"I thought you'd want to know that I found out what Skete Jackson has—or had—against you and me," I told Sonny.

I explained about the right-of-way and Reese's scheme to get Skete to sell. Sonny seemed unsurprised. "I figured it was something like that," she said.

"Well, I guess the good news is that now that everybody got what they wanted, there won't be any more trouble."

The minute I said it, I knew how naive it sounded. If the projected development proceeded as planned, the future would hold *nothing* but trouble. Sonny didn't bother pointing that out to me, and I was grateful.

She said instead, "Can we talk about something else for a second?"

She glanced at the row of chairs behind me. "You look like you're ready to fall over, and I know I am. Shall we sit for a minute?"

I glanced around for Maude. "I didn't drive myself."

"Just for a minute," she insisted, and I knew she wasn't just offering me a chance to rest.

She sat almost as stiffly as I did, and we smiled at each other as we arranged our crutches. Then she

grew serious. "Raine," she said, "I wasn't going to say anything to you about this. I know you're not entirely convinced about this animal communication business. To tell you the truth, neither was I until you came to see me yesterday."

I frowned uncomfortably, glancing again around the room. "Listen, Sonny, that's all fine and well between you and me. I mean, I can stand a little eccentricity now and then. But these people trust you. You might even say they have a stake in your—well, competency. Are you sure you want to be talking about this here?"

She gave a rueful shake of her head. "A couple of weeks ago—a couple of days ago—I would have agreed with you. Fun is fun, but I'm a lawyer, and the future is at stake." Her eyes met mine. "Do you know what the prognosis for my kind of arthritis is?"

I shook my head.

"It's not very good, I'm afraid. I'm skating on the edges of technology right now, trying to stay one step ahead of it. But in another couple of years I'll be looking at heavy opiates to control the pain, liver damage, cognitive dysfunction, virtual paralysis. In other words, not exactly the quality of life I enjoy now. In fact, not much life at all."

I swallowed hard, not knowing what to say.

She straightened her shoulders and smiled. "So. Facing something like that, you tend to make odd choices. Things that might seem important to others

aren't all that essential anymore—things like what people think of you, for example." She gave a little chuckle. "Who knows? In my case, being taken for a crazy incompetent might even be a kind of advantage.

"I told you the other day that I'd always thought of this thing I had with animals as kind of a game. Sometimes it worked; sometimes it didn't. Maybe it was genuine; maybe it wasn't. What difference did it make? But when you told me about what you found"—her gaze turned inward and became troubled—"I started to think maybe it was more than a game. Maybe it was . . . important.

"So." She took a breath. "Here's the thing. You can believe me or not. But this is what I think. No, it's what I know.

"You asked me if Cisco knows where that little girl is," she said. "I told you he didn't. He still doesn't. But he says the border collie knows."

I closed my eyes slowly. *Great*, I thought. *Just great.*

"And I don't suppose she, um, the border collie, that is, is inclined to share that information?"

Sonny shook her head, looking distressed. "I'm sorry."

Maude touched me on the shoulder. "Are you ready, my dear? We still have dogs to exercise." She looked at Sonny. "Very nicely done, Ms. Brightwell. I suspect you have a long fight ahead, and I wish you luck."

"I wish us all luck," Sonny said, looking at me.

"Did you learn anything from the worthy opposition?" I inquired as Maude and I made our way out into the night.

"Nothing we didn't already know. This company—Calan-Wells Development, quite an exclusive firm, you may have heard of them—is ready to close escrow on Hawk Mountain as soon as the estate clears probate. I couldn't discern quite how much money was involved, but when I guessed three million, he laughed in a way that made me think it was quite a bit higher."

"Yeah, but these things take ten, twenty years."

"Quite often. But I received the impression—"

"Wait a minute." I stopped a few feet before the car and stared at her in the pinkish glow of the overhead streetlight. "What did you just say? About probate?"

"Well, my dear, even Reese Pickens can't sell land he doesn't legally own yet."

"What do you mean—yet? I looked at the plat book just today. It said PICKENS right there, just like it always has."

"Of course it did. The Pickenses have owned that mountain since . . ." And then her eyes widened a fraction. "Oh, but of course, you're too young to remember. Hawk Mountain never belonged to Reese—it was his wife, Ellen's. She deeded it over to her sons in trust when Luke was born—probably to make certain they had an inheritance. Reese was rather dis-

solute back then, and no one ever thought he'd amount to much, and Ellen was from a nice family— land rich and dirt poor, as they used to say. Your father drew up the papers on the transfer of deed. The odd thing is—and your father and I talked about this a good deal—I don't think anyone ever bothered to tell Luke that he owned half a mountain. By the time Ellen died, Luke was already skidding down the slippery slope, and I imagine Reese decided what the boy didn't know wouldn't hurt him. In fact, I don't suppose he ever would have found out if . . ."

And we both understood at the same time. "If the development company hadn't come looking for him," I finished for her, "to offer him a couple of million for his share."

"Right."

We stood gazing at each other in the semidarkness for a time, and then I asked, almost reluctantly, "When Luke's brother was killed ten years ago, what happened to his share of the mountain?"

"It reverted to Reese, the trustee parent, since the boy was a minor at the time of his death."

So at the time negotiations began, Reese only owned half the property in question. The other half was under the control of his angry, violent and estranged son.

And now the son was dead.

A shiver of wind raced down my spine, and I hunched inside my coat. "Let's go home," I said.

Chapter Fourteen

Okay, so maybe Reese was right. I might not be quite as smart as my daddy was, at least when it comes to unraveling the intricacies of the criminal mind. It's a well-known fact that I didn't inherit my mother's charm, either. But even I, given enough time and provocation, can start putting two and two together and come up with the right answer.

It was all a matter of focus. I guess it's only natural to assume that when a murder and a kidnapping take place at the same time, in the same place, and involving the same people, the two incidents are related. But what if they weren't? What if Luke's murder had nothing to do with Angel's kidnapping?

As any good tracking dog knows, it's all about the search grid. I had been looking for answers in the wrong places, while the real reason Luke was

killed had been staring me in the face, morning and night, for most of my life. Hawk Mountain.

And the worst of it was, I was very much afraid that the only witness to the crime had been sleeping in my boarding kennel for the past three nights.

All right, so I had known—or at least heavily suspected—from the beginning that the border collie belonged to Reese Pickens, which I suppose made me guilty of dognapping. He had bought a pair of border collies from a reputable breeder of working dogs a couple of years ago, at the same time that he purchased a flock of sheep. Arrogant cuss that he was, he assumed he could train a pair of herding dogs himself, and he didn't come to me for help until the male dog had chased down and killed one of his sheep. I recommended a highly qualified herding instructor, but Reese never called her. A week or so later, the male dog was found tied to a tree and shot through the head.

When confronted by a representative of the humane society, Reese Pickens told her that what a man did with his own damn dog on his own damn property was his own damn business—although I suspect the expletive he used might have been a little stronger than "damn"—and charged her to get off his land and to never return.

So that's why I hadn't been exactly proactive about returning Sonny's border collie to her rightful owner. And, if I hadn't needed the little dog as an

excuse to pay Reese a visit today, I would have made sure that she never set paw on his property again.

We were usually open all day on Saturday for pickup and delivery, but it was the slow time of the year, and we didn't have anyone scheduled. When Maude called to say she thought one of her dogs had pulled a shoulder muscle and she needed to get him to the vet for some cortisone, I told her I was closing early and not to worry about coming in. That's all I told her. She would not have approved of what I was about to do, and she probably would have been right.

I needed to have a good look around Reese Pickens' place. And if I got caught snooping, fortunately I had just the excuse.

The border collie sat eagerly when I unlatched her gate, her eyes alert and watchful. I said, "Come on, sweetie, we're going to go for a ride." I looped the leash around her neck and she didn't object. "But don't you worry, I'm not going to leave you there. Not in a million years. I just need you to help me out with something, okay?" I stroked her under the chin and she regarded me with that keen watchfulness that is the border collie's trademark. It could be downright spooky, if you didn't know the breed characteristics. "I'm not going to let anything bad happen to you, I promise. Do you trust me?"

And the funny thing is, I think she did. She got to

her feet and walked to the open gate of the kennel, trailing the leash behind her, and waited for me to catch up. Like I said, spooky.

I was tired of the crutches, small surprise, and today had decided to abandon them, which was only one of the reasons I was glad Maude wasn't around. The decision almost proved to be a disastrous one when, as I opened the gate that led from the backyard to the side yard, where the car was parked, Cisco came barreling through the dog door and almost knocked me off my feet. The border collie jerked her leash out of my hand and the two of them took off on a mad dash through the gate and around the yard.

I yelled something that probably shouldn't be heard by sensitive canine ears, and certainly should never come out of the mouth of a positive-motivational dog trainer. I slammed the gate shut and drew in a breath to call out something more appropriate, and probably equally as ineffective, like "Here!" or "Down!" but the two of them were in the zone now, oblivious to all but each other and the pure pleasure of running. Cisco was a fast dog, but that border collie was a race car. It was hard to resist the temptation to stand in awe and watch her go.

While they circled the oak tree and leapt the boxwoods and cut ninety-degree corners around the garden shed, I hobbled over to the car and, without uttering a single word, I had Cisco racing toward

me with the border collie close behind. He skidded to a stop before me, tongue lolling, grinning happily up at me. All I had done was open the car door.

"Oh, all right, you renegade," I told him and swung the car door open wide. "You can come."

A more disciplined trainer would have sent him to his crate with a good scolding, but I didn't have time. Besides, I still didn't have hold of the border collie's leash, and she didn't look nearly as anxious to jump into the car as Cisco did. I figured she would follow him in, and I was right.

When Hanover County was first opened up to settlers in the mid-eighteen hundreds, four families grabbed the best parcels of land in the fertile valley between two mountain ranges—the Stocktons, to whom I am indebted for my legacy; the Petersons; the Hanovers, who are way back in Buck's family tree; and the Pickenses. Land tends to stay in families up here, and we all still lived pretty much where our ancestors had planted us. Though our parcels were big and separated by dips and elevations, and though when the leaves were on the trees not one of us could see the chimney tops of the others, the county road connected us, and no driveway was more than five miles from mine. I got to Reese Pickens' battered rural mailbox in less than eight minutes.

It looked as though a tornado had been through the woods on either side of the rutted dirt drive.

Trees lay like broken matchsticks across the bare forest floor. There wasn't enough damage to call it a timber operation—when those vultures came through they left a swath of ruination behind that could be seen for miles—but this certainly wasn't the result of a natural phenomenon.

I had gone about a hundred yards, bouncing up a hill and around a corner, when I got my answer. The path was blocked by a huge backhoe and a pile of gravel at least two stories high. I hit the brakes hard, spewing mud.

The backhoe driver was standing beside his machine, warming himself over a cup of coffee. He ambled over to me when I rolled down the window.

"Mornin'," he said. "You here to see Mr. Pickens?"

"Yes. What's going on?"

He shook his head. "I told him he should've put a sign down by the road."

Cisco poked his head through the open window and gave the man a big welcoming doggie grin. Fortunately, the stranger liked dogs.

"Pretty golden. I got me a couple of labs at home." He ruffled Cisco's ears. "We're leveling out the drive, here, widening it, putting down the gravel for paving come spring," he told me. "We got the trees down last week, but yesterday was the first day it was dry enough to get the dump truck up here with the gravel."

"Wow," I said. "Sounds like a big job." And why not? Reese Pickens was about to come in to a lot of money. Why not spend it?

"Oh, yeah; it's gonna take two, three weeks before we get the heavy equipment out of here. Then he's gonna bring in the landscapers, the stone masons—he's putting in a big gate down at the road with stone columns and whatnot, gonna be real pretty. But meantime, you gotta go around if you want to get to the house."

"Go around?" I began, and then I stopped short, feeling like an idiot. Of course. Most people used the man's driveway when they wanted to get to Reese Pickens' house—which, in fact, very few people did. But there was another way in. Reese used it to transport livestock from his back pasture, or sometimes, rarely, to get hay in and out in bad weather. Some of the locals called it Old Quarry Trail—who knew why. It was otherwise known as Buck's driveway.

"Thanks," I said and put the SUV in reverse. "Stay warm, now, you hear?"

"I'll try, ma'am. Bye, big fellow." He gave Cisco a final scratch on the ears and lifted his hand to me as I backed carefully out the way I had come.

I cursed myself for a fool all the way back down the county road, and I actually hunkered down in my seat as I turned into Buck's driveway, hoping he wasn't at home, or was at least asleep as I passed by.

Situations like this happened a lot in the mountains. The cost of grading out a road or a driveway was such that two, or even three or four, families would often share a single drive. Or public roads, by virtue of being too narrow to accommodate real traffic, would eventually morph into private drives. Since Buck's mother's house had been the only one on that little dirt drive for more than seventy years, it was easy to forget that it actually was a road that led somewhere. And where it led, approximately half a mile after Buck's small clapboard house, was to a sharp left turn up a rocky, washboard trail that ended, less than a hundred yards later, at Reese Pickens' barn.

Cindy Winston had not been returning from my husband's house the other morning. She had been coming back from Reese's. I knew it in my bones.

The border collie began to whine anxiously as I pulled around the barn and into the yard in front of the house, and Cisco barked sharply. I flinched and snapped, "Cisco, quiet! What's the matter with you? You don't bark in the car!"

But apparently he did bark in the car, and he proved it four or five times in rapid succession. The border collie's agitation grew, and she paced back and forth across the rear seat, tail tucked and head down. Cisco's excitement was only a reaction to her distress.

I reached my hand over the seat and opened my

palm to her, murmuring reassurances. "It's okay, girl, I swear. You're okay with me. I'm not going to let him have you."

Cisco barked again and actually pawed at the window. I told him impatiently, "Stop that!" He was not doing my already strung-tight nerves any good.

It appeared that Reese was serious about doing some remodeling. There was a big commercial Dumpster in front of his house, filled to overflowing with construction debris, and a tarp over the back portion of the roof.

Reese's truck was not in the carport, but that didn't mean anything. He had more than one vehicle, and he might be out checking stock, or conferring with his construction crew about whatever other projects he might have planned for his newfound wealth. To be on the safe side, I blew my horn. The border collie barked sharply in alarm, which of course set Cisco off. I covered my ears against the brief cacophony and commanded in a tone of voice that never failed, "Dogs! Quiet!"

They quieted, but Cisco wriggled his way so eagerly toward the door that I had to hold him back with one hand while I opened the door. When I got out and shut the door again, he flung himself into the driver's seat and put both paws on the window, panting after me anxiously. I scowled at him. "What in the world's the matter with you? Sit down and behave yourself."

I looked around cautiously and called, "Reese?"

There were old sofas, chairs and floorboards piled all around the Dumpster. Apparently Reese was not only remodeling, but redecorating as well. I cautiously circumnavigated the house, which was a plain board-and-batten construction that probably dated back to the nineteen twenties, and discovered that a foundation had been poured for a sizable addition in back. It was easily twice the size of the current house, in fact, and from the way the roof was gutted I could guess he planned to add on a half story as well.

He certainly was building a lot of house for just one person.

I stepped around pallets of construction materials that were tightly covered with tarps and a few inches of hard-frozen snow where they were placed in the shade. The mud around the house was frozen too, and I guessed that construction had been halted for at least a week. Maybe he'd had the decency to stop work when his son had died. Or maybe the weather had simply held him up.

In contrast, the surrounding yard was packed dirt; I had been here in the spring and knew for a fact that nothing grew there. The fences were patched with kennel wire and the barns had holes in the roofs. There was an old toilet and a refrigerator in back of the barn that had been there since the Carter administration. Reese clearly was not house

proud. So what had caused him to suddenly decide to spend his fortune on expanding and upgrading his domicile?

There was only one thing I could think of, and it was so twisted that, when applied to the Pickenses, it actually made sense.

In order to avoid a pile of roofing material, I had to squeeze close to the house. As I did, I could have sworn I heard something inside—a television? A radio? My stomach tightened and I thought, *Oh great, he's home after all.* And I was about to be caught prowling around Reese Pickens' house. I'd be lucky if he didn't shoot me.

To lend myself legitimacy, I called out again, "Hey, Reese? It's me, Raine Stockton!"

No reply. I walked casually to the side door and banged on it. Still no reply. And I couldn't hear the television anymore. Maybe it was on a timer. I shrugged and started back toward the car, and that was when I could have sworn I saw a flash of movement through the window at my shoulder. Someone was inside. *Oh, crap,* I thought, *I really am going to get shot.* If he was in there and he wasn't answering my hails, the best thing I could do was leave, and quickly. Among the many things Reese Pickens was known for was his temper.

I was hurrying around the corner of the house when I heard tires crunching on the barely graded road by which I had just come. The dogs started

barking furiously from inside my car as the truck crested the hill. It was definitely Reese's pickup, and I cast a confused glance back toward the house.

But I didn't linger. I made it to the Explorer before Reese slammed his truck into park beside me, and I stood by the door with my hands shoved into my pockets, trying to look casual and confident while my heart was slamming against the back of my throat.

Reese got out of his truck and came around to me. He was wearing a leather cap and an expression that would have frozen boiling water. He said, "Miss Raine."

"Hey, Reese." My breath fogged the air and I tensed my muscles inside my parka because I didn't want him to see I was shivering. "I was just looking for you."

He cut his eyes from me to the two dogs, who were now sitting in the front seat of the Explorer. Cisco scratched the window with both paws, his panting breath steaming up the glass.

Reese said, "Yeah, they told me at the site there was some woman headed up here. Never dreamed it would be you."

I took a breath. A deep one. "I see you got rid of your sheep."

"Yeah. Damned nuisance. Sold the whole flock to some fellow over in Cantwell. "

I gave a little start as I remembered what Sonny

had said about getting her sheep from a man in Cantwell. "Lionel Perkins?"

His eyes narrowed suspiciously. "Yeah, that's right. How come?"

I shrugged and lied gamely, "Everybody knows he buys sheep."

But involuntarily I glanced back at the border collie in the front seat of my truck. Holy cow. Could that little thing have followed her own sheep across the mountains to Sonny Brightwell's house? Well, why not? Dogs had certainly done stranger things. And no wonder she had been, as Sonny had put it, "obsessed" with the sheep. If they were hers, she must have been overjoyed to have found them. She must have felt as though, after all she had been through, she and they had finally found a home.

I turned back to Reese, trying very hard to keep my expression neutral and my tone casual. "Guess you don't need a dog then."

He just glared at me.

"Because someone turned in this little girl"—I jerked my head toward the border collie, who was huddled near the passenger door—"a couple of days ago. I thought I recognized her as yours."

There was a tense, pulsating silence. My fist clenched around the keys in my pocket. I was prepared to cut and run if he made any claim of ownership. But sometimes I could read people almost as well as I could read dogs. And I knew that Reese

Pickens was not about to demand the return of this dog, even to spite me.

Or at least I *hoped* he wouldn't.

At last he said gruffly, "Yeah? So?"

"So I need you to sign a release, if you don't mind, so I can put her up for adoption." I held his eyes steadily. "I mean, you don't want to keep her, do you?"

"Hell, no. Crazy bitch, she's been nothing but trouble since I got her. Never was any good on sheep. I should've taken her out and shot her months ago."

I deliberately ignored that remark and opened the door to the SUV, pushing Cisco out of the way. The smell of warm fur and doggie breath greeted me as I stretched across the seat to retrieve a standard release form from the glove compartment. Cisco, sensing my tension, whined anxiously and actually tried to climb over me to get to the door. I shoved him back. I attached the form to a clipboard and handed it to Reese with a pen.

"Just sign at the bottom," I told him, amazed at how steady my voice sounded. "It says you're releasing the dog to me. I'll fill in the rest later."

He grunted as he took the clipboard from me. "You gonna pay me anything for her? Damn dog cost me five hundred bucks."

I watched him handle the pen awkwardly with his bandaged hand. At least I had the sense to wait

until he'd begun to scrawl his signature before I said, "How's the hand? Dog bites can be painful, I know."

He shot a sharp look at me from beneath iron gray brows, and the final loop of his signature tore the paper. I reached for the clipboard and held it tight against my chest. She was mine. She was safe. And now that I didn't have to worry about the dog, a sense of reckless courage surged through me, and I forced a friendly smile.

"Boy, you're really doing some work around here, huh? It's going to be nice."

He said nothing.

"I guess that's what people do, though, when they come into money. They spend it. I know I sure would."

"It ain't none of your concern what I do with my money, or my place."

"That's true enough," I agreed pleasantly. "I was just wondering, though. You took an awful big chance, didn't you? Hiring all these contractors, ordering the materials, and the whole deal could've fallen through at any minute. I mean, what if Skete Jackson hadn't caved?" I drew a breath. "What if Luke hadn't died?"

His brows drew together sharply. "What the hell are you talking about?"

I shrugged, trying to look disingenuous. I was very bad at it. "I mean, here you were, going to all

this trouble and expense on the promise of selling property you didn't even own. It doesn't make sense." Then I made my eyes big. "Or maybe you *did* own it, or thought you were going to. Maybe you got Luke to sign it over to you, or promise to. Maybe that's why Mr. Marrit's office was doing a title search. These things take time. And then what happened? Did Luke change his mind?"

Here it was, all my courage, and all my stupidity. Behind me, Cisco made a low, growling, whining sound in his throat, and for some crazy reason that made me feel safe. I had my dogs with me; I could do anything.

I said quietly, "Did he find out whose name Cindy had put on Angel's birth certificate, Reese? Is that why he changed his mind, and is that why he went over to Cindy's house raising hell? Because he found out you were the father of her baby?"

A kind of darkness came into his face, and although he did not move or make a motion toward me, he suddenly seemed larger and closer. And I was afraid. He said in a low, rumbling voice, "I think you better get yourself on out of here, Raine Stockton. And I think you better do it now."

I shivered inside my coat and I couldn't have agreed with him more. Suddenly, more than anything in the world, I wanted to get back into my truck and get out of there as quickly as I could.

And that was exactly what I would have done

had not Cisco, as I opened the driver's door, suddenly barked excitedly, once, and scrambled past me, out the open door, and around the car.

I cried, "Cisco!"

He looked back at me happily, barked again, and bounded onto the raggedy old sofa that was leaning up against the Dumpster. Leaving the car door open, I rushed to grab him, but I was too late. From the sofa he scrambled onto the armchair that was stacked on top of it with a surefootedness I had never seen on an agility course, balanced there for a moment with his front paws on the edge of the Dumpster, and then pulled himself up and over.

I cried again, helplessly, "Cisco!" as he leapt into the Dumpster.

The border collie was barking madly and Cisco had disappeared beyond the rim of the Dumpster. I knew there was construction debris in there, sharp nails, broken glass, who knew what else. How was he going to get out? What might happen to him before he did?

I moved around the front of the car toward the Dumpster as quickly as I could, and pulled myself up onto the old sofa, thinking I could climb up the same way Cisco had. But the sofa shuddered under my weight and lost a leg. The armchair that was on top of it toppled sideways and onto the ground. I barely jumped aside in time, and I landed on my

bad leg with a stab of fiery pain that drew a cry from me.

I heard Cisco barking from somewhere over the rim of the giant box. Grabbing my thigh just above the knee brace—as though that could somehow diminish the pain—I took a few staggering steps back and, to my relief, I could see a snatch of golden fur. That meant that the Dumpster was almost full, and he hadn't fallen very far. I shouted to Reese, without turning around, "Get me a ladder!"

This I said to the man whom I had only a moment ago all but accused of murdering his own son. The thing is, I was genuinely surprised when he didn't comply.

"Damn it, Reese!" I swung around to look for a ladder but found something closer—a weathered one-by-six board that might have been used for siding, or even decking. I propped it up against the base of the hill on the long side of the Dumpster and found that it just reached the top of the box. I gave the board a cursory shake to test its security, and I prepared to climb up to save my dog.

I think I may have registered the sound of tires on gravel, some place distant in the background, but I barely noticed. Because just as I put my two hands on either side of the board in preparation for hauling myself, throbbing knee and all, up the incline, I saw Cisco's head appear on the far side of

the Dumpster. He was holding something in his mouth.

I was so relieved to see him that at first I didn't register what he was holding, nor why his tail was wagging so madly. He had managed to get his front feet on an old door that was lying kitty-cornered across the two back sides of the Dumpster, and his back feet had found purchase on an old TV. All I had to do was move the board to the other side of the Dumpster, and he would be able to climb out himself.

"For heaven's sake, Reese, will you help me move this thing?"

He did not reply and I didn't wait for him. I bit down hard on my lower lip to take my mind off the volcano in my knee as I dragged the board around to the other side of the Dumpster and propped it up firmly so that one edge met the door—just like a dog walk.

That was when I realized two things. The first was that Cisco, with his front paws on the "bridge" formed by the door and his back paws digging for purchase on the slippery casing of the television set, was paralyzed with fear. He wasn't going anywhere. The second thing I noticed was what Cisco had firmly clasped between his jaws.

"Oh, my God," I whispered.

It was battered and stained, stiff with frost and

spikes of sawdust, but it was impossible to mistake: a fuzzy pink bunny slipper.

"Cisco," I said softly, holding his eyes. "Good find, boy. Good find." He wagged his tail again, looking proud and satisfied and, when he saw the distance between himself and me, very worried.

"It's okay, boy," I urged. I put my hands on the board again and started up to him, but it was a foolish idea at best. I could not even swing my injured leg onto the board. "Cisco, come here, boy." There was desperation in my voice now. "Come on."

Behind me Reese said coldly, "Get down from there, Raine."

I didn't take my eyes off my dog. I could hear the border collie barking maniacally now, and, yes, that was the sound of a car coming closer. I said firmly, "Cisco, now. Here!"

He whimpered in a way that all but broke my heart, and I could see his jaws clamp down even more firmly on the treasure in his mouth as he summoned up all his courage and, toenails scrabbling, he pulled all four feet onto the door. There he froze, shaking and looking at me helplessly.

"Good boy, Cisco!" I exclaimed. I held out my hand to him, although he was still a good eight feet away. "Bring it to me. Good boy!"

Reese said, "Get away from the goddamn dog, Raine."

I shot him an angry look, and then my breath

dried up. Reese was standing by the open door of his pickup truck, and in his hand he held a hogleg .22 pistol. A lot of people carried them in the glove boxes of their farm vehicles for rattlesnakes, coyotes and the like. It was not, perhaps, the most efficient weapon on the market, but it would definitely serve its purpose at this close range.

I backed slowly away from the Dumpster. Cisco watched me go with a low, slow-wagging tail and confused eyes. I made myself not look at him. "Where is she, Reese?" I said. "Where is Angel?"

"You just couldn't mind your own business, could you?" His voice was matter-of-fact, and he pulled back the hammer on the gun.

With a confidence I was very far from feeling, I said, "You're not going to shoot me, Reese. Not over this."

He looked at me as though seeing me for the first time, and a little smile flicked at his lips. It seemed almost genuine. "Shoot you? Of course not." And he raised the gun, pointing it at my dog.

Chapter Fifteen

Buck's truck spattered gravel against the fender of the Explorer as he pulled in behind my car. He got out without closing the door, and he stopped. Reese didn't look around.

Buck was not in uniform. He wasn't even wearing a coat. But he had his service revolver in his hand, held close to his thigh. He said, "You want to put that gun down now, Pickens."

Reese said, very calmly, "A man's got a right to defend his property from trespassers and stray dogs. You stay out of this if you want to keep your job."

I said, very quietly, "Cisco found the other slipper, Buck. Angel's slipper. It was in his Dumpster."

"Is that a fact?" Buck took a step toward Reese.

"Just stay back there, Deputy. Both of you need to just back off. I don't want anybody getting hit by a

stray bullet." Reese made a small jerking motion with the gun, although he kept it aimed squarely at Cisco. And Cisco, crouched on top of the Dumpster and unable to move, was a plain-sight target.

I took a stumbling step back from the Dumpster, and another. I said calmly, "Cisco, drop."

Cisco released the slipper. And he didn't move.

Reese laughed. "Too little, too late, missy." One eye narrowed as he took elaborate aim.

It all happened at once, but every detail was crystal clear. Buck rushed toward Reese, but he was too far away; he didn't have a chance. I swung my shoulder toward Cisco, I lifted my arm, I thought, *You can do it, boy. Just like we practiced.* I shouted, "Cisco, walk it!" And Reese fired the gun.

The border collie charged from the car in a black-and-white fury, a flash of fur and sharp canines, a roar of snarling and staccato barks. From the corner of my eye I saw the dog take Reese down, and the gun flew from his hand. Cisco streaked past my head, down the plank and across the field, and the border collie was close behind.

No matter how loudly I shouted, neither one of them looked back.

I sat on the tailgate of the Explorer, shivering and swallowing back the tears that pounded at the back of my throat. I didn't want any of the half dozen cops who swarmed all over Reese Pickens' house

and yard to see me cry. And I sure as hell didn't want Reese to see.

My throat was raw from calling for the dogs, and I had fallen over some stubble in the field, bruising my hands and doing who-knew-what damage to my knee. I was scared. I was cold. I was in pain. But most of all, I just wanted my dogs back.

Buck sat beside me, pried my fist out of my coat pocket, and tipped two pills into my hand. "Codeine," he said.

"Where did you—"

"Don't ask, don't tell."

I dry swallowed the two pills gratefully, trying not to choke. It wasn't easy.

Buck said, "We've torn that house inside out. Outbuildings, basement, even sifted the hay in the loft."

"No sign of her?"

"Signs, yes. A pair of pajamas, a storybook . . . no Angel. No way of telling if she was here for a night or a week or even if she was here at all. I mean, those things could belong to some other kid."

"She was here," I said. "They were hers."

"Probably." His voice was very sober. "Roe has gone to pick up Cindy from work. If she can identify the items we found, if they're Angel's . . ." He expelled a breath. "Looks like we're going to have to search the Dumpster."

I closed my eyes tightly and the word that escaped me was barely a moan. "No . . ."

"All this construction around here . . . a freshly poured foundation . . . Let's face it, Raine, a body could be buried anywhere."

I shook my head fiercely. This I refused to accept. "No," I said again, more strongly, almost angrily. "She's not . . ." My nostrils flared on the quick, short breath of cold air I inhaled and then puffed out forcefully. "You don't have to search the Dumpster. Cisco wouldn't have left her there . . . we would know if she was there."

"Cisco's not a cadaver dog," Buck pointed out gently.

"It doesn't matter." My voice was as tight as the muscles at the back of my neck, and they were like iron. "She's not dead." We had not come all this way to find a body in a Dumpster. We just hadn't.

"I hope you're right, hon. I really do." And then he added, "Either way, we've got enough to haul Reese Pickens in for kidnapping. Thanks to Cisco."

"He was just doing his job," I said softly. "He was told to track the other slipper, and he did . . . through the woods, to the root cellar . . . to here. He got his target. He's a good dog."

Buck rested his hand on my shoulder briefly. "Yeah," he agreed. "He is."

I swallowed hard to clear the thickness in my throat and swiped at my eyes with the back of my

hand. I forced something like a smile. "And how about that little border collie, huh? I guess she saved Cisco's life."

And, if anything Sonny said was right, the border collie had known where Angel was all along. She had known because she had seen Angel, right here, the night she had run away. The night that a loud noise, like thunder—or a gunshot—had frightened her, and she had bitten Reese Pickens.

I shivered. After this, how could I ever doubt Sonny again?

Buck said, "They're both smart dogs. If they're not already at your back door, they're on their way."

Once again I tried to smile. I had called Maude, and even now she was pacing through the woods surrounding my house, calling the dogs. They could be on their way home. Sure they could.

I drew in a breath but couldn't quite make myself meet Buck's eyes. "Look. I owe you an apology. Yesterday, I lit into you for no reason, and if there had been a reason"—I dragged my eyes to his and made myself sit up straight—"it was wrong. I was wrong. I'm sorry."

He looked at me for a moment, almost as though debating whether to accept my apology. Then he said, "Yeah, you were wrong. About a lot of things. But then, so was I. I started putting things together after I saw you yesterday, and realized Cindy must've been coming back from Reese's place that

morning you saw her car. Then I saw you drive by this morning, and it made me curious. So I called Maude. She told me about Reese putting Skete up to throwing that bomb. I figured you were coming up here to start some kind of trouble, so I thought I'd ride on up and try to calm things down. Guess it's good I did."

"I guess." I cut my eyes to him. "You brought your gun."

"There might've been varmints."

"Only one."

He said quietly, "We're not complete idiots down at the department, Raine. Cindy Winston has been a suspect in Luke's murder from the beginning. But you have to be real careful in cases like this. Real careful. We didn't know where Angel was, remember, or if she was even alive, or being held hostage to keep Cindy quiet, or what. You can't go charging in with barrels blazing when there's a child's life at stake."

I swallowed hard. "So you knew about Hawk Mountain?"

"According to Frank Marrit, Luke was ready to close on the sale of the property to his father for ten thousand dollars."

I whipped my gaze around to him. "Ten thousand? Reese must've had an offer of millions for it!"

"Luke was a junkie, Rainey. What did he care beyond his next fix? Then something happened. He

called Frank up on Tuesday, mad as all hell, telling him the deal was off and he could burn those papers. The next thing we know he's over at Cindy's and, well, you know the rest."

Not all of it, I thought, and I slid to the edge of the tailgate, gripping Buck's arm to get my balance as I stood up. The codeine was starting to kick in and it didn't hurt too much. "I need to look for the dogs."

Buck held on to my elbow, partially to steady me, mostly to stop me. "Come on, Rainey; it's Cisco. He'll come back."

I shook my head. "They were scared to death, running wild. Who knows how far they'll get before they even stop to look where they are. And the little one was wearing a leash. She could get snagged or—"

I couldn't go on about how close to the highway we were, or about predators or poisons or men with guns. "I need to find them."

"I can't leave now. I'll help you look as soon as—"

"Goddamn it, this is a goddamn illegal search!" Reese's voice cut furiously across the busy yard. "I'll have your badges for this, every last one of them! And you can't use a goddamn thing you find here, do you hear me? Not a thing! Anybody could have put that shoe in my Dumpster and you know it! This whole thing is a setup and I'll see every damn one of you in jail before I'm done! Take your goddamn hands off me!"

He jerked away from the deputy who was trying to lead him toward a parked patrol car. The officer said, "Mr. Pickens, all we want to do is ask you a few questions. Now, we can sit down and talk like friends right here, or—"

The sheriff's car bounced over the rutted hill and pulled in at a sloppy angle between two patrol cars. Almost before the vehicle had stopped moving, Cindy tumbled out, still wearing her Waffle House uniform, her teased-up hair windblown and her face streaked with mascara. She plunged across the short expanse of frozen mud to Reese and she grabbed his arm. "What have you done with my baby?" she screamed. "Where is Angel?"

Reese turned to her, and in that moment, for just a glimpse, I saw a Reese I had never imagined existed before. From the angry bull he had been an instant ago he seemed to shrink before a mother's terror. The florid color drained from his face and left it gray; his silver hair was tangled by the wind, his shoulders slumped. He looked, for the first time since I had known him, old.

He said hoarsely to Cindy, "I don't know."

Her voice was wild with fear as she cried, "What do you mean, you don't know? You promised you'd look after her; you said she'd be safe! Where is she, you bastard, where is she?"

I think I breathed then for the first time in almost an hour. "You don't have to search the Dumpster," I

repeated to Buck, "and I don't think you get to arrest Reese Pickens, either."

I pushed away from him and started toward Cindy. "You can't charge a man with kidnapping when he was just looking after his own child."

Cindy tore through the house, calling for Angel. She returned to the yard and cried, "Angel, you come here to mama right now! Angel, do you hear me?"

Suddenly Cindy saw Reese again and she turned on him, pounding his chest with her fists. *"Where is she?* What did you do with my baby? This is all your fault, all of it! What did you do with her?"

This is why Uncle Roe is a good cop. He didn't go barging in there asking questions, though heaven knows there were plenty of them to be asked. He just stood there, a little to the side, and let the drama unfold. So did I.

Reese caught Cindy's flailing fists, shoving her away. "I didn't do anything with her! You think I would do something like that? She took off! How the hell should I know where? I was out of the house for just a minute. I told her to hide if anybody came up. She's got to be around here somewhere."

"She's *not* around here somewhere! Do you think the cops would still be standing around here if she was?"

It was about that time that Reese realized what he had said and who had been listening. And that

was when Uncle Roe stepped in. Hands in pockets, he walked over to Reese and nodded toward the patrol car. "Why don't you and me have a little talk?"

Cindy sat on the steps of the house, shivering and weeping in great, ugly gulps. The police had sealed off the house, so I had gone to my car and gotten a blanket for her. It was covered in dog hair, but Cindy didn't seem to notice. And I've got to tell you, at that moment I regretted every mean and nasty thought I had ever had about Cindy. No one should have to suffer like that. No one.

I sat on one side of Cindy, Buck on the other. Between us, Cindy hugged her knees and rocked back and forth, a cigarette burning untouched between her shaking fingers. "That bastard, that bastard," she said. Tears were streaming down her face and her voice was taut. "This was his stupid idea. It's all his fault. I never should have trusted him, never!"

Buck opened his mouth to speak and I gave him a warning look over Cindy's head. If he pushed her now, it would be all over. Fortunately, we had done this before, and he trusted my judgment.

I said gently, "I don't think he'd hurt Angel, Cindy, I really don't. I think she just wandered off, like he said. And there's still plenty of daylight and dozens of policemen out looking. They're going to find her."

She raised eyes to me that were red and swollen

and stark with desperate hope. "Where's your dog? Can't you go get your dog?"

I swallowed hard and actually couldn't speak for a moment. So Buck put in, "We've called for dogs. But we're going to find Angel long before they get here."

Cindy choked back a sob and pressed the back of her hand hard to her mouth. Cigarette smoke burned my eyes.

I said sympathetically, "I guess it was the car Reese gave you that tipped Luke off, huh? About what was going on between you and Reese?"

Cindy sniffed and released a shaky breath and, to my surprise, seemed actually relieved for an opportunity to talk about something else. She took a drag on her cigarette and an inch of gray ash tumbled off. "I guess. I don't know. Luke was—he was crazy. He was—he tried to hurt my baby. That's why we broke up. But he kept coming back, wouldn't leave me alone."

"So you went to Reese for help," I supplied. "Is that when you told him Angel was his daughter?"

She brought the cigarette to her lips again, her gaze fixed on the sheriff's car where Reese Pickens sat in the backseat, door open. Roe was still interviewing him.

"Are they going to arrest him?"

"I don't know," Buck said. "Do you think he should be arrested?"

She took a final drag on the cigarette and tossed it away. "He didn't want nothing to do with us, all these years—he could've helped out a little. But then when he finds out Luke is interested, well, it's all, 'Let's build a house, let's get married.' I think he just wanted to piss Luke off."

"And so that night," Buck said gently, "after Luke found out about you and his daddy, he came over to your house with a gun. You scuffled over the gun, and you got shot. What happened next, Cindy? What really happened?"

She fumbled for the cigarettes in her pocket with one hand and pushed her tangled hair away from her wet face with the other. "God, it was such a nightmare. Such a freakin' nightmare. I didn't even know I was shot until he dragged us out in the yard. He forced me and Angel into his car. He—"

"Drove you over here," I finished for her, and Buck looked surprised. "He wanted to confront Reese. He probably threatened you, or Angel. But things didn't go the way he planned, did they, Cindy? Somebody got the gun away from Luke and killed him. That was how Reese got bitten by the dog. When the gun went off, the dog attacked him."

She stared at me, an unlit cigarette poised before her lips. "How did you know about the dog?" she asked. Her voice sounded small and confused, just like she looked at that moment.

My heart was pounding hard, but I didn't dare

stop now. "You had to get rid of the body, and the gun. So you and Reese put Luke in the back of his own pickup truck and hauled him out to Three Mile Creek. You dumped the body down the ravine, and you were about to throw the gun away, but then something went wrong. A patrol car spotted the truck. You had to separate. It wasn't that far for Reese to walk back to his house, and you and Angel headed for the closest shelter—the old Peterson home place."

Cindy lit a cigarette with shaking fingers. "Stupid," she said on a breath. "It was stupid from the start; I knew it. But I had a baby to take care of. What was I going to do?"

"You could have called the police," Buck suggested, not entirely kindly.

She shook her head sharply. "No. No, I couldn't."

"You were hiding there in the cellar while we searched the place," I said quietly. "And when we were gone, you took off for Reese's place. He probably drove you to within a few hundred feet of your mother's house, and you pretended you'd been walking all night. You figured Angel would be safe with him, especially after he closed up his driveway so people couldn't get in and out. You left the gun behind in the cellar on purpose, but I'm betting you didn't even realize Angel had dropped her toy."

Cindy shuddered inside the blanket, exhaling a quavery stream of smoke.

"It must have been hard on you," Buck said, "keeping up the pretense, watching your friends and neighbors searching for Angel, worrying your mama . . . knowing all the time she was safe and sound with Reese. And it's not like you were being a bad mother. You spent every minute you could over here with her." A quick glance at me over Cindy's head. "But what was the point, Cindy? You couldn't keep her hidden forever. Why did you keep us all looking like that? You could have just brought Angel home with you that morning and told everybody you'd escaped. Why pretend she'd been kidnapped?"

But I knew the answer to that one. "Because little girls can't keep secrets very well," I said softly. "And Angel had witnessed a murder."

Cindy whispered, "Oh, God. Oh, God help my baby."

"Who killed Luke, Cindy?" Buck asked gently. "You or Reese?"

Cindy turned to me, her eyes dark with turmoil and pain. "I did what I had to do, don't you understand that? I did what I had to do to protect my little girl! Isn't that what mothers are supposed to do?"

I nodded, my throat tight, feeling helpless. "You did fine, Cindy," I said.

She gripped my arm, hard. Her voice was rising on the edge of hysteria. "You find my baby, you

hear me? She's out there in her sneakers and dark is coming on and you need to find her!"

I looked across her head at Buck, and we both knew the interview was over.

I wrapped my arm around a porch rail and pulled myself awkwardly to my feet. "We'll try, Cindy," I said, looking bleakly out over the shadowy mountains. But this time, I didn't have much hope.

I couldn't even find my own dog.

Chapter Sixteen

Maude put me on house duty while she searched the woods and the fields, cruised up and down paved roads and dirt trails, and knocked on every neighbor's door within a four-mile radius of where the dogs had disappeared. It was frustrating and infuriating to sit helplessly at home, waiting for the dogs to show up, but I knew Maude was right. She could cover more ground than I could, and if they came home and no one was here, they might take off again.

The entire police force was once again out looking for Angel Winston. Only one person was looking for two lost dogs. And I couldn't do a single thing to help either search.

I called Sonny Brightwell. After all, the border collie had followed her sheep there once. It wasn't unreasonable to think she might do so again. I

briefly filled her in on the details of the afternoon, and her voice was quick with concern as she volunteered, "Do you want me to come over? Can I help you look for them?"

I was filled with gratitude, but I knew that she would not be any more useful on a cross-country search than I would. "Thanks," I said, "but it's getting dark, and I think"—I had to pause to clear my throat—"I think we're going to have to wait and start again in the morning."

I hesitated. "You were right," I said. "The border collie did know where Angel Winston was. You were right about a lot of things. I don't suppose—"

Sonny responded quickly, "They're together. That's all I know. I don't think either of them is hurt, but they're worried about something. I'm sorry, Raine. That's all I'm getting. I know it's not much help."

"No," I admitted. "It's not." And then I smiled a little. "Do you want to know something funny? Your sheep—they turned out to be part of the flock that Reese Pickens sold to that Lionel Perkins in Cantwell. The border collie used to work those sheep, and she must have a really strong work ethic because she followed them all the way to your house. I wouldn't be surprised if she turned out to be a great sheepdog."

Sonny was silent for a long time. I thought I

heard a little thickness in her voice when she spoke again.

"Maybe," Sonny offered uncertainly, "it would help if you thought like your dog. Why did he run away, instead of running to you? Where would he go if he was scared? What does he want?"

But that was the trouble, wasn't it? I couldn't think like Cisco. If I could, I would have trusted him from the beginning. He ran away because he didn't trust me either, and for a dog trainer—for anyone who loves a dog—there is no more cruel truth.

As for what he wanted . . . he just wanted to do what I asked him to. He just wanted to be a good dog.

I asked Sonny to call her neighbors, just in case anyone spotted a loose border collie, and I hung up the phone.

I went over to the mantel, which was filled to overflowing with trophies, photographs and framed title certificates. Overhead I had strung a length of twine between two nails, and attached to it was a colorful array of ribbons, most of them blue, from dozens upon dozens of different shows and competitions. In the center of it all was the oil portrait of Cassidy, her beautiful blond fur tousled in the breeze, her gaze fixed on a distant horizon. I looked at it for a long time.

Slowly, I took the portrait down and rehung it on the "dog wall" in the dining room, where I dis-

played framed snapshots and action shots of all my other dogs—the puppy pictures, the funny pictures, the Christmas card pictures. The ribbons, titles and trophies I took down and packed away in one of my mother's fabric-covered hat boxes, where I could take them out and look at them from time to time.

On the hook where Cassidy's portrait had been I placed an action shot of Cisco clearing the bars on the triple jump—ears flying, forelegs extended, grinning with the sheer exuberance of success. There was only a handful of ribbons and two framed title certificates to replace the ones I had removed, but that just meant there was plenty of room left for the ones we had yet to earn.

I touched the glass that covered Cisco's photograph, tracing the curve of his ear, the beautiful line of his back. I closed my eyes slowly.

"Oh, Cisco," I whispered. "Come home. Just, please . . . come home."

Buck called. He sounded weary and tense, and the frustration crept through in his voice. "Déjà vu all over again," he said. "Not a sign of Angel. We tossed the Dumpster. We're scouring the woods. Pickens is sticking by the story Cindy told us—that Angel was with him, hiding out, until you showed up this afternoon. He says she disappeared while he was away from the house, trying to stop you from finding her. Damn it all to hell. You want to know

something weird? Now he says he killed Luke. Claims it was an accident, of course. The gun went off while they wrestled over it. First Cindy confesses, now he does. Jesus, you don't think they could really love each other, do you? And they're trying to protect each other?" He paused. "Any sign of the dogs?"

"Nothing yet." I was trying hard not to sound as discouraged as I felt. "Is Reese in custody?"

"They both are, until we get some answers." Again a silence, and when he spoke once more his voice was heavy. "If we don't find Angel tonight, we're going to start digging up his backyard come daylight."

My insides twisted like a dishtowel wrung to dry.

Half an hour after dark, Maude came in. I could tell by the look on her face that she had no good news, and the shoulders of her peacoat were glistening with drops of rain.

Lost dogs often mark their trail so that they can find their way back home. But rain washes away the scent, and the trail would be lost.

"Not unusual," Maude said, briskly shaking the droplets off her coat. "They haven't been gone that long, only a few hours really. It's not time to worry yet. And with all the people searching around the Pickens place, I would be very much surprised if

someone doesn't spot them before morning. Cisco is a big baby, and he's not going to want to spend the night in the rain without his supper. He'll go to the first person he sees; you know that. I don't suppose you've heard anything about the little girl?"

I shook my head, trying not to look as depressed, or as frustrated, as I felt. "Buck says both the parents—I mean Reese and Cindy—are being held, whatever that means. They still think she might be . . . I mean, that Reese might have . . ."

Maude said briskly, "Don't be absurd. If there were a corpse in that Dumpster, or anywhere on the property for that matter, Cisco would have let you know. After all, he tracked his quarry all the way there, didn't he?"

Maude did have a way of getting straight to the point, and I smiled wanly, wanting to believe her.

Headlights flashed on the windows and we both tensed, hurrying to the door. I didn't know whether to be relieved or disappointed when, a few minutes later, Sonny made her way up on the porch, her raincoat held over her head, using her umbrella as a crutch.

"Sorry," she said when I opened the door. Her hair was tousled, her face was dotted with rain, and her expression was wry and resigned. "I couldn't stay away. I thought if you had one more person looking, we could cover a little more ground. After

all"—she took a deep breath—"it's my dog out there."

I wanted to hug her. In approximately one more second, that's exactly what I did. "Come in," I said, and my voice was muffled by more than her shoulder.

I stepped away and swiped a hand over my face, trying to look normal. "Maude just got back. She's been searching all afternoon."

Sonny stepped inside just enough for me to close the door, but she looked anxious to be going. "I have flashlights," she said, "and about a gallon of coffee. If we get started right now, we can backtrack to where they were lost. It makes sense that they would be headed home, doesn't it?"

Maude said, "A lost dog travels in an ever-diminishing circular pattern toward home. I covered most of that grid this afternoon."

"But you don't know how big a circle they started with," Sonny was quick to point out.

"No," admitted Maude, "I don't."

Sonny caught her bottom lip between her teeth and looked at me, then, uncertainly, at Maude. Then she looked back to me again. "Listen," she said in a voice that was low, almost as though she did not want Maude to hear. "It's probably nothing, but . . . I don't know, when you said what you did about the sheep, and the border collie following them all the way to my house . . ." Again she bit her lip, and

for the first time since I had known her, she actually looked embarrassed. "It's just that I got the feeling . . . when I was trying to reach out to her . . ." She looked at me, her eyes beseeching. "Is there anyone around here who keeps sheep? Because I got the distinct impression—I swear she said to me that she had found the lost sheep."

I looked at Maude questioningly, and she shook her head, a little impatiently, I thought. I answered Sonny. "Well, there are some people with sheep, but they're way on the other side of the county. I don't think they could have gotten that far—"

Suddenly I stopped, everything inside me suddenly congealing into a crystal-sharp moment of clarity. It felt like a jolt of electricity, and it froze me in place. *Think like your dog*, Sonny had said. *She's found the lost sheep.*

I turned slowly to Maude, feeling stunned and breathless. "Oh, my God," I said, "I know where they are."

Maude parked the car sloppily at the edge of the rutted tracks, headlights on high beam and angling wildly through the pattern of trees and misty raindrops. "Raine, are you sure?" she demanded worriedly. "This is an awfully long way from Reese Pickens' house—"

"No, it's not," I interrupted her, flinging open the door. "It's all downhill, a straight shot."

Even before I was out of the car Sonny had flung open the backseat door and was stumbling out. It was rough terrain and no place for someone with a disability—didn't I know it. But I did not try to stop her. No one could have stopped me.

I drew my hood up over my head and plunged out into the rain, switching on my flashlight to join Sonny's beam. "Border collies," I told her, "herd everything. They think they're in charge of anything smaller than them. A lot of people say that they treat the children in the family like—"

"Sheep," Sonny said softly, sweeping the woods with her light.

Maude came up beside us. "We should have called the police."

"Bring the phone."

Maude's flashlight beam joined ours. "In my pocket. But I still don't know what makes you think—"

"This is where Angel would have come," I insisted. I grabbed Maude's arm for support as we started down the rain-slick hill. I could barely drag my injured leg beside me, but the pain was a distant thing, hardly worth my notice. "Her mother told her she was safe here. Maybe she couldn't have made it by herself without getting lost, but she's got the dogs. Cisco didn't run away from me," I told her urgently. "He ran *after* Angel. He was still tracking!"

"Raine, I'd like to think you're right," Maude

began unhappily, and suddenly Sonny, who had been walking beside us, stopped.

"Listen!" she whispered.

For a moment there was nothing but the sound of rain spattering on the hood of my coat and dripping on the undergrowth. And then I heard it. My eyes went to Sonny, and we both met Maude's startled gaze triumphantly.

It was the bark of a dog.

We pushed through the slapping branches and tangled roots, flashlights bobbing crazily, taking the same path I had taken only two days before to the log cabin in the woods. A black-and-white border collie was crouched on the threshold of the building, barking furiously.

Maude said sharply, "That'll do, girl," and the border collie silenced, wagging her tail uncertainly.

Sonny stumbled forward, making small choked sounds in her throat that sounded very much like words. "Sweet girl, here I am; you're safe now; I'm here!" And as she reached her, the little border collie jumped into Sonny's arms and began to lick her face. I heard laughing, and crying.

I cried, "Cisco!"

A single sharp bark filled the silence left by the border collie. An alert bark. A find.

Maude went to Sonny as the border collie wriggled excitedly out of her arms. She caught hold of the leash the dog was still wearing and ran her

hand through her fur soothingly. I pushed past them, stumbling, almost sobbing, and swung my flashlight around the room. My beam hit a flash of phosphorescent eyes, a golden shape—and something else. The white moon shape of a dirty, frightened face. Over the sound of my pounding heart I could hear soft sobbing.

Angel Winston was huddled in a corner of the building, her arms around the neck of my big golden retriever. When I turned the flashlight on them, she buried her face in his fur, weeping. Cisco turned his head and licked her ear.

"Good dog, Cisco." My voice trembled. "Good, good dog."

I bent down as much as I could to put myself on the child's level as I approached. "It's okay, honey, we're here to help. You're safe now. This is my dog; isn't he beautiful? He's been looking for you all this time, and now he found you. Isn't he a good dog? Don't cry. It's okay now, really. You're safe."

Behind me I heard Maude saying on the phone, "We need help at the old Peterson place. We've found Angel Winston. No, she seems to be okay . . ."

I gently put my arm around Angel's thin, wet shoulders, and Cisco wiggled madly with happiness. But she just cried harder and dug her fingers into Cisco's fur. "It's okay, honey, really, you can let go of him now. Your mommy's real worried about you, and we're going to take you home."

She shook her head violently, and finally turned her tear-streaked face to me. "I c-can't! I can't go home. I did a bad thing, a real bad thing, and I have to hide."

I glanced over my shoulder toward Maude for help. "You didn't do anything bad, sweetie. See how much Cisco likes you? What could you have done that was so bad?"

She looked at Cisco, and her grip relaxed a little on his fur, even though the tears did not slow. She dropped her eyes. "I shot the bad man with a gun," she said. "I shot him dead."

Chapter Seventeen

"I cannot believe," Maude declared as she set a tray holding my mother's Fostoria pitcher and matching iced-tea glasses on the wicker side table, "that they let Reese Pickens go, just like that."

"Well, he was never really charged with anything," Buck pointed out, "and neither was Cindy. The inquest determined an accidental death."

Maude sniffed disdainfully. "And I'll never believe that. I don't care what that poor, scared little girl said."

We all looked at one another for a moment in silence. No one was inclined to disagree with her.

March had given us a surprise spring day, with temperatures in the seventies and sunshine bouncing off every surface. In honor of the occasion, Maude had made the season's first pitcher of sweet

iced tea and served it on the front porch—because, she said, invalids needed fresh air.

And invalid was exactly what I was since returning from the hospital three days ago. Actually, the arthroscopic surgery on my knee had been an outpatient procedure and not worth nearly all the time I had spent postponing it. I had been off the pain pills the second day and could already get around better than I had been able to do before the surgery. But that didn't mean I didn't enjoy the pampering.

So I had let Buck carry me out to the wicker chaise on the porch, and I didn't protest as Maude propped pillows under my knee and draped me with a quilt. Nor did I object too much to the homemade tea cookies and savory cheesepuffs that were served with the tea, nor to the stack of magazines and newspapers that had been solicitously placed on the table for my perusal. I particularly liked the newspaper that featured the front-page photo of Angel Winston with her arms around a big, grinning golden retriever. Headline: HOME AT LAST.

I said thoughtfully, "Okay, so maybe it happened like Cindy said at the inquest. Luke was waving the gun at his dad, and Reese knocked it out of his hand. I can see that. Reese is a hotheaded old bull and Luke was drunk enough to lose his grip on the gun. And so maybe Angel picked up the gun and Luke tried to grab it from her, and maybe it went off, the way Cindy testified—"

"*Maybe* being the operative word," Maude put in dryly.

"What I don't understand is why they didn't call the police right then. Why not claim it was accidental, or even self-defense? Why dump the body, and then try to hide poor Angel and pretend she was kidnapped?"

"I'll tell you why," Maude said. "Because it wasn't Luke who tried to get the gun from Angel; it was Reese. Maybe the gun discharged accidentally, but most likely it did not. And given the history between them—the land deal, the rivalry over Cindy—Reese would have been taking an awfully big chance on any jury believing that the shooting was accidental."

This was, in fact, the prevailing theory among those in the know. When questioned, all Angel could say was "the man" tried to take the gun from her and she had shot "the bad man." Whenever anyone tried to get more specific, she became hysterical. The court-appointed child psychologist would not allow Angel to testify at the inquest, so Cindy's testimony, and Reese's, were all the judge had to go on. And, of course, they had had plenty of time to get their stories straight.

Buck said, "Well, there was no fingerprint evidence, so we'll never know for sure."

"I still say it was a stupid thing to do," I countered, "dumping the body. And what about the fact

that they both confessed to killing Luke before the inquest?"

"Actually," Buck reminded me, "Cindy never confessed. She just said she 'did what she had to do.'"

"But Reese did confess."

"Right. And he later testified that he only said that to protect Cindy and Angel. In fact, that's what they both ended up saying under oath, about why they dumped the body, and about why they lied under questioning. They were trying to protect Angel."

"Cindy didn't really believe they would put a six-year-old in jail," Maude demanded.

Buck shrugged. "More likely foster care. Single women like Cindy, marginally employed, are always worried the state is going to take their children away from them. That's probably how Reese talked her into leaving Angel with him in the first place."

"And what *is* social services doing for the little girl, may I ask?" Maude wanted to know.

"Counseling, I think. Parenting classes for Cindy."

"It still makes no sense to me," Maude said, pouring more tea. "Were they going to keep the poor child hidden forever?"

Buck took another cookie. "You want to know my opinion? I think Reese was waiting for us to get

fingerprint evidence back on the gun. He was pretty sure he'd wiped his prints, but what if he hadn't? He probably had a backup plan to leave the country. We found an up-to-date passport and twenty-five thousand in cash in his house, but that doesn't prove anything. On the other hand, he had a strong motive for staying—several million of them, as it turns out—so if the gun came back clean they could bring Angel back, probably with a little coaching about where she'd been, and there would be no hard evidence to point to him. The last thing he needed, though, until he knew for certain whether the gun was clean, was to have Angel testifying about the fight between him and Luke."

"That's crazy."

"We're talking about Reese Pickens, here."

"So. He gets to collect his millions on Hawk Mountain and live happily ever after."

"Looks like it."

"I don't know," I said thoughtfully, gazing out over the blue-gray shadow of Hawk Mountain that loomed from my backyard. "I know Reese is a nasty old coot and rotten to the core, but I kind of think he was starting to feel like a father to Angel. When she was lost—really lost, I mean . . ." I shrugged. "He couldn't fake that. I'd like to believe that it all happened just the way Cindy claimed, and that both of them were really just trying to protect Angel from losing one, or maybe both, parents,

not to mention having to testify in court and be harangued by the media." Again I shrugged, a little embarrassed by my own sentiment. "I don't know. I'd just like to think that."

Both of them looked at me skeptically for a moment, then Maude reached across and patted my hand. "Good for you, my dear. And, who knows, maybe you're right. After all, according to rumor, Reese has agreed to pay a more-than-generous child support and set up a college trust fund for Angel."

"After his paternity became part of the court record," Buck pointed out, "he didn't have much choice."

"Still, it worked out nicely for Angel and Cindy," I said. "They'll be able to get a real house in town and Cindy won't have to work so much. Maybe she could even go back to school or something." I hesitated and glanced at Maude. "And, you know, I was thinking . . . when they get settled in and all, with a fenced yard, of course, maybe we could call around to some people and see about getting Angel a dog. A golden. I think it would be good for her."

Maude practically beamed at me, and Buck looked at me so tenderly that I blushed. He said, "That'd be real nice, Rainey."

I added quickly, "Of course, we'd have to give her some lessons in pet care, and she'd have to come every week for obedience classes."

"Of course," Maude agreed, still beaming.

The dogs, who were scattered all over the porch, came to a sudden alert at the sound of tires crunching on the driveway. All, that is, except Cisco, who remained in a perfect down underneath my chaise, his head upturned toward me in rapt attention, ever hopeful of a dropped crumb. I smiled at him and flipped him my cookie. Maude gave me a reproving look, but I didn't care. Cisco deserved a little pampering too.

"And speaking of which . . ." Maude got to her feet as the white van pulled into the turnaround in front of the house. "Right on time, I see," she noted with approval.

I waved as Sonny got out of the car, followed almost immediately by a bounding black-and-white dog. Of course all of my dogs rushed off the porch to greet them, and for a moment Sonny was lost, laughing, in a melee of wagging tails and happy sniffing.

"Sonny is starting obedience lessons today with her new dog," I explained to Buck. Then, "Magic, Cisco, here! Majesty, Mischief!"

I rewarded them each with a snippet of cookie as they came to me, and they soon lost interest in the new dog. Cisco was the last to leave, but then, he had a preexisting relationship with the border collie. They had been through a lot together.

The transformation in Sonny was really close to miraculous. She moved with a lightness of step and

a grace that completely belied the fact that, less than two weeks ago, she had been in a wheelchair. She took the steps two at a time, and when she reached out a hand to ruffle Cisco's fur, I noticed that the swelling in her fingers was almost gone.

"Wow," I said, "you look great."

She laughed. "You know, they say that dogs have a healing power. Frankly, I think it's just the fact that trying to keep up with this young lady gives me the exercise I was missing before. And what about you? How are you feeling?"

"A lot better than before the surgery," I answered.

I introduced Sonny to Buck, who had gotten to his feet like a gentleman the minute she approached, and almost at once he had her engaged in an easy, friendly conversation about the old buffalo farm, and her life on the coast before she had come here, and the development of Hawk Mountain. No wonder women liked him. It wasn't charm that he had, so much. It was that he was just plain nice.

Sonny turned to me, her expression somber. "I saw the surveyors as I drove up. It looks as though they're marking off access roads across from your driveway."

I stared at Buck accusingly. "You didn't mention that when you came in."

"It doesn't mean a thing," he assured me. "They have to have a good survey before they can close on

the land. It doesn't mean they're actually going to start cutting down trees anytime soon."

"But if they're surveying right across the road from me—"

"He's right," Sonny said quickly. "We have plenty of tricks up our sleeve before we give up on this."

I relaxed, mostly because I wanted to believe her. But almost like a premonition, the sun dropped a fraction behind the peak of Hawk Mountain just then, and the shadow it cast over my house chilled me to the bone.

I drew the quilt up to my chest and held out my hand to the border collie. She crept close to sniff my fingers, and I scratched her gently under the chin. "What did you decide to name her?" I asked.

"Mystery." Sonny grinned. "As in 'It's a mystery to me how I ever let her go in the first place.'"

"How's she doing with the sheep?"

"We're working it out. But I'd still like her to have some herding lessons someday."

"I'll see what I can do."

"Well, Maude is waiting," Sonny said. "We'd better go."

"Stop by for some tea before you leave," I invited. "I'll catch you up on all the gossip."

"Sounds great." She waved happily to me and let Mystery pull her down the path to the kennels.

Buck and I sat in silence for a while, sipping tea

and munching cookies. Cisco stretched out in a patch of sunshine between us, looking as content as it was possible for a dog to look with a plate of cookies he was not allowed to have only three feet from his face.

I said, "I'll be starting back in tracking class as soon as I get mobile. I guess you'd better put me back on the SAR emergency contact list."

Buck slid a gaze my way, a smile tugging at his lips. "Already done."

I tried to look stern, but before I could reprimand him for leaping to conclusions, he protested, "Come on, Raine. You're good at this. You've got an instinct—and I don't mean just for tracking. We need you on the force."

"Yeah, well," I returned wryly, "you come up with a way to pay me and you just might have yourself a deal."

"I'll bring it up with the man in charge. Meantime"—he reached across and snagged my pinkie finger with his own, gave it a swing and released it—"it was good working with you again."

A smile began to spread over my face that I could not prevent, and, before Buck could think it was entirely directed at him, I glanced down at Cisco. "I have a good dog," I said.

"You have a *great* dog," he corrected. Then, gently, "Welcome back."

This time I met his eyes, and I let him see me smile.

It wasn't long before the tenderness of the moment embarrassed us both, and Cisco, ever sensitive to our moods, provided the perfect distraction by rousing himself to drop a tennis ball into Buck's lap. We both laughed, and Buck stood up, chucking the tennis ball across the yard. Cisco raced after it and Buck ran down the steps, with the other dogs in hot pursuit, for a rousing game of fetch.

It was a good day, the kind you want to remember when the wind howls and the snow swirls. I knew winter wasn't over yet and the days of shirtsleeves and tennis balls were still weeks away, but that was what made this picture, of man and dogs romping across the patches of winter sunshine, so precious—something I wanted to hold on to.

Okay, so maybe I was wrong about Reese Pickens. Maybe that moment of grief and terror in his eyes had been entirely fake, and maybe he had coldbloodedly murdered his own son for the price of a mountain and had used Cindy and Angel to cover his guilt. Maybe justice had not entirely been served; maybe there were still evils in the world that needed attending to, but weren't there always? In the meantime, Angel Winston was safe, both from the dangers of the wilderness and from the bad man who had tried to hurt her. Her mother would have enough money to take care of her, and

no matter what mistakes she had made in the past, even Cindy deserved that much.

Cisco left the game to come bounding up the steps to me, panting happily through a mouthful of soggy tennis ball. I leaned over and took his face between my hands, laughing and ruffling his ears. I felt good. Mystery the border collie had found a home. Cisco was here, and everywhere I looked there were happy dog faces. Spring was right around the corner, and, with it, the first agility trials. My surgeon predicted I would be running again by fall, but I planned to be back in the game much sooner than that.

After all, my dog and I had a lot of work to do.

Read on for an excerpt
from the next
Raine Stockton Dog Mystery,
coming in December 2006

There is a cliche that every boy who has ever been to high school knows: If you're looking for a wild time, your best bet is the preacher's daughter. Well, if you think she was trouble, you ought to check out the judge's daughter.

That would be me.

Even though my father has been dead for almost ten years, and even though I am a full-grown woman who has been away to college and opened her own business and been married and everything, most people still think of me, not as Raine Stockton, Grown-Up Woman, but as Judge Stockton's Daughter. That's what happens when you live in the same small community all your life—it's hard to get away from your past. And, like most kids who for whatever reason are held to a higher standard than others,

I guess I always felt I had a lot of past to get away from.

I don't mean to imply that I was promiscuous as a teenager. I'm sure I didn't have any more fun than any other girl in a county whose full-time population is less than three thousand, whose county seat doesn't have a movie theater, roller rink or bowling alley, and whose Saturday night entertainment options are decidedly limited, if you know what I mean. The teen pregnancy rate is quite a bit above the national average in our little corner of the Smoky Mountains, but I'm happy to say I beat those odds.

The truth of the matter is, I've really only loved two men in my whole life, and I fell in love with both of them in high school. The first one grew up to be deputy sheriff and a sterling asset to our little community of Hansonville, North Carolina. The second spent more time in trouble with the law than out of it and has now been a fugitive from justice for over ten years. Guess which one I married?

Wrong. I actually married Deputy Sheriff Buck Lawson. In fact, I married him twice. And most days I'm still not certain I made the right choice.

Currently Buck and I live apart, although we haven't quite gotten around to untying the knot for the second—and most likely the last—time. For one thing, it's all just too embarrassing. First you're married, then you're not, then you're married

again. No one likes to make a mistake, but to keep making it over and over again—that just makes you look like you haven't been paying attention. For another thing . . . Well, I suppose that "other thing," which neither one of us can quite put into words, is the real reason we stay married even though we can't bring ourselves to live together.

As for Andy, the one who got away—literally—he was actually one of the reasons my marriage started to fray the first time. But it's not what you might think. Approximately six months after Buck and I were married, the local headquarters of a petrochemical plant were bombed, and four people died. Buck, along with a good portion of the known world and every federal officer who cared to go on record, thought Andy was guilty. I thought he was innocent. It's never good for a couple to discover that early in a marriage how passionately they can disagree over something that fundamental, and when the argument is over an old boyfriend . . . Well, as I said, that's never good. Perhaps even worse is the fact that we never got to find out which one of us was right. Andy Fontana outwitted both the local and the federal authorities and fled the country before he could be arrested, and in the process became something of a local folk hero. No one has ever seen or heard from him since.

Until, that is, the first day of June, in the year I call my Summer of the Bear.

Praise for *Smoky Mountain Tracks*

"An intriguing heroine, a twisty tale, a riveting finale, and a golden retriever to die for."

—Carolyn Hart, author of the
Death on Demand and Henrie O series

"Combines a likeable heroine and a fascinating mystery, along with an education about the great contributions of search and rescue dogs . . . told in a crisp, engaging style."

—Carlene Thompson, author of *Share No Secrets*

"*Smoky Mountain Tracks* has everything: wonderful characters, surprising twists, great dialogue. Donna Ball knows dogs, knows the Smoky Mountains, and knows how to write a page-turner. I loved it."

—Beverly Connor, author of the Diane Fallon
Forensic Investigation Series